UNLEASH YOUR INNER TUDOR

Henry VIII's Inspirational Guide to a Completely Sizzling, Sparkly, Tyrannical, Much Wider, Demanding, and Sexier You

by King Henry VIII
@knghnryviii

Cover illustration: Nick Cann

ISBN: 9781521912065

Some of the relationship advice herein appeared in a previous ebook titled, Monarch of Your Bedchamber. *It appears here as well as a favour to you. You're welcome.*

Table of Contents

Chapter 36 – Sex, Mistresses & Other Bits
Following the Date of Your So-Called Death

Epilogue

Foreword

Henry VIII – the warrior, the poet, the hunter, the joust winner, the legend, the All-England Swan-Eating Champion 1509 -1542.

Henry VIII – he of the fine singing voice, fantastic pair of legs, brilliant mind, and the biggest boobs in Christendom.

Henry VIII – the seducer, the intriguer, the woo-er, the hot boyfriend, the sexy lover, the fantastic husband, the champion of women's issues.

On the subjects of love, laughter, leadership, parenting, diet and exercise, and motivation, believe me ladies and gentlemen, this monarch knows it all – and more! – and is eager to do a complete dump of inspiration on you. (Am I phrasing that right? I'm trying to sound modern.)

As his second wife, the Henry VIII I knew was just getting started! I cannot *wait* to read this book to learn a few life tips myself! This is going to be epic!!!

-- Anne Boleyn*
Signature authenticated by a great number of experts & witnesses who were not paid by the author

Rules for Peasants Reading This Book

1. Whilst reading this glorious and inspirational guide to life, a full prostration upon the floor (face down, arms outstretched) is preferred but a kneel is okay. But do it with feeling. And don't try one of those half-hearted one-knees-bent poses! Kneeling means both knees!

2. One must read this inspirational guide to life aloud in a booming, authoritarian voice (this applies to all situations whether one is in bed alone or with company, upon a horse, in a restaurant, or on public transport).

3. At the commencement of each reading of this glorious book one must stand and in a loud, stentorian voice sing the following song -- and do *not* try to riff sing it like you're bloody Beyoncé. Pick a note, the proper note, and stay with it. Don't go frantically searching about the scales for Christ's sake:

God save our sexy king,
Ruler of everything,
God save the king!
Make him notorious,
Obese and glorious,
Heir-makingly Tudorious,
God save the king!!!!!

An Introduction from This My Very Pen

Why have I written this inspiring guide to life?

Because you need it. You people need this book like a mouth needs wine. Like a musical needs a song about wishing for things. Like an axe needs a neck. And I think you must know you need it because the question I get constantly on Twitter is: "@knghnryviii, how can I be more like you?"

Well. That's a huge ambition. Like a sneeze that sings of wishing to become a typhoon.

If one is to span the unimaginable distance between who I am and whatever you are at the very least, it's going to require a book-length effort. The task of writing such a volume would drive a lesser man to madness.

But lesser men are not Tudor monarchs.

Thus I am here, dear modern reader person, to do the herculean task of guiding, Tudorsplaining, and, one hopes, shaming and frightening you into becoming the best Henry VIII you can be.

Because of the clear magnitude of this tome, it deals with life's biggest, most impenetrable, and universal questions such as:

- How can I avoid eating vegetables?

- Can I be sexy whilst not being obese? (Hint: no)

- If I have a daughter or two who expresses nothing but ill-will and abhorrence for me, is that normal?

- What are the sexiest ways to woo a lady with my shirt off?

- How can I select a wife with the right sort of womb?

- What if my wife gives me a girl and my mistress gives me a boy?

- My dad wishes to marry the same girl I want to marry – help!

- Which foods will best manage my moods? And in what tonnage?

- There's a lady I wish to wed and her husband is almost but not quite dead – OMG what ever shall I do?

- How does a man become more than a man? An icon? A myth?

Fortunately for you this book does not simply ask such penetrating questions and leave you to sort it out for yourself, no, no, this book provides answers – specific steps you can and must take to achieve your goals.

Unleash Your Inner Tudor even offers life hacks for ladies because whilst most have not been taught to read (this is still the case, I assume?) and are solely focused on the needs and demands of the men and children in their lives, somewhere deep inside, ladies want answers to things just like other people.

Look, I'll be the first to admit that to the untrained eye my start at becoming Henry VIII could seem rather unplanned, random, simple luck even. And some of it is, to be perfectly frank, the result of divine accident.

I was told by my mother (or maybe an angel told me in dream, I can't recall) that when God made me it was the morning after some dodgy take-away the night before and a bit too much Shiraz from a box. Whilst fumbling about in his glorious, heavenly solarium where he performs wondrous deeds our lovely Lord God Jehovah knocked his person-making supplies about, spilled things, blended things with eyes half-closed and poured the man-batter into his big glowing 3-D printer. There came a noise like the universe splitting in two, a knocking, a slurping, and a hey nonny nonny. A cloud of glittery smoke later, there I was. Dripping in glory. The one, the only.

Leader, husband, father, king, bacon machine, visionary.

Our Old Darling Divinity has since tried, I am told, to reproduce these results and thought he almost had it with Rob Ford. Then with Donald Trump – better luck next time America.

So with the recipe unknown, the mould broken, the original blue prints missing, can you really and actually hope to be at all like me?

Whispers *It's not bloody likely, is it?*

However, saying it's unlikely that you, sweet reader, can achieve true Tudorliciousness would be to imply that this book is pointless, which cannot be true as I am writing it. And in fact this book very much has a purpose and a point as we shall see.

Rather than discourage you, I will say instead take my bejewelled hand and together let us embark on a journey of laugher, love, leadership, violent mood swings, a dash of psychosis, and irresistible Henry VIII magnificence.

Pay attention, take notes, stop checking arsing Snapchat every 30 seconds, and you may learn the secrets to unleashing the me that is inside you (in the almost entirely non-sexual sense).

Chapter 1
My Childhood – An Extremely Short Chapter

Tudor Life Tip: Children aren't born cruel, violent, or sociopathic. So it takes an exhausting amount of neglect and callousness to prepare them for leadership!

Dear everyone who writes books about themselves,

I always skip the bits about your childhood. It's boring. You knew nothing. You did nothing. You simply ate food, made noises, and got larger.

I'll be a role model here and keep this brief. This is everything you need know about my early life. My father was Henry VII, whom God had made King of England by successfully doing nasty stabbing things to Richard III on the battlefield at Bosworth Field in 1485. Which is why I like God so much.

My mother was Elizabeth of York, who might have married Richard III but didn't. And wouldn't have anyway and never had any physical contact with him and if you say she did I shall have your eyeballs pulled out through your nostrils.

Dad married Mum mostly because she was A) pretty, B) extremely nice, and C) it's hardly worth mentioning but a tiny bit because she was the daughter of Edward IV (a Plantagenet king!! ☹), and gave dad and his heirs greater legitimacy throne-wise. This last bit is maybe three to five percent of why he found her to be good wife material.

My mum and dad got on beautifully and did what a royal couple is supposed to do which is to create a dynasty – mostly involving the production of male children. My conceited and lugubrious brother Arthur was born first and he was to be king. I came along later and I had two sisters who aren't important. One we married off to the Duke of Suffolk and the other was pushy and opinionated and dad sent her off to Scotland, which provided me with a useful template for how one handles difficult ladies (more on these strategies later).

What we have learnt in Chapter 1

- Have you ever wondered why in the Bible there are no chapters about the childhood of Jesus? Now you know.

- Childhood is simply the drawbridge to the castle of adulthood. No one reads books about drawbridges.

- Difficult ladies – that's why Scotland exists!

- Is it just me or is there something so satisfying about short chapters?

Chapter 2

Chapter 2 has been abandoned thanks to an incident of inexcusable violence. See Chapter 3.

Chapter 3
An Introduction to Tudor Family Life &
Thoughts on Chapter 2

Tudor Parenting Tip: If given the choice between castrating dragons with tweezers or having daughters, go with dragons.

I've had to give Chapter 2 a miss. I thought it would be instructive to have my son and heir, Edward VI, contribute a chapter to this volume. He got off to a pretty scholarly start on how he'd recently learnt the difference between things we eat, such as cheeses, and things we do not eat, such as ponies. And hats.

He is six, I should mention.

Oh, and he went on for a bit about how his odd-looking, ginger, half-sister Elizabeth once made a codpiece from an actual cod.

Whilst writing this, his other half-sister, Mary, strolled into the room, read his scribblings over his shoulder, and began shrieking at full lung-strength, enraged that Edward hadn't mentioned a thing about her. She has remained in a massive strop after being compelled to sign a document saying my marriage to her mother (Catherine of Aragon) was complete bollocks, thus cutting Mary from the line of succession to the throne, and made a bastard, which is, let's be honest, such a girl thing.

As always, attracted by the sounds of chaos and discord, Elizabeth flew into the room and for reasons we haven't yet untangled began instantly to hurl books and delicate, royal break-y things at both Mary and Edward, making Edward cry and prompting Mary to respond by grasping Elizabeth by the throat and trying to push her out a window.

In moments like these, as a parent, it is ideal to have a well-trained military force at your command.

When the guards cleared the girls out, little Eddy said he did not wish to finish writing his chapter as he was now fearful of his sisters. Poor lad. I took him on my lap and he asked me why girls are so mean and scary.

I told him it's because they're evil.

He gave me a hug.

What we have learned in Chapter 3
- Most of your children, especially if they're girls, won't like you for unknowable reasons and you can't focus on that too much
- When possible hire henchmen to deal with your kids
- Hugs not drugs

Chapter 4
How to Be a Tudor – Getting Started

Tudor Life Tip: Begin each day by making a list of the things you must do. Do all the sexy bits. Never do the boring bits.

Have you noticed what you've already learnt? Probably not so I'll spell it out. A Tudor refuses to be bored or boring. Here is my typical to-do list of a given morning:
- brekkie
- archery
- falconry (note to self: do not eat falcon!)
- wenching
- go to treasury, roll about in my Pope plunder until lathered in sweat whilst wearing only gold underpants (cardio!)
- invent the English Renaissance
- have someone beheaded
- stampede through throne room ("presence chamber" for you history nerds) shouting "THIS MEANS WAR!"
- debase coinage
- make Parliament wet selves
- quite nearly invent steam-powered transportation/decide to do later
- strum lute sexily
- impregnate a lady
- cake

Notice what's missing? All the stupid, boring bits. Think on it. There may be a quiz later.

Chapter 5
A Quiz

Ha! I've taken you quite by surprise. Here is my glorious "What We've Learnt So Far in This Book" Quiz. (Circle the correct answer.)

A Tudor never does what?
A.
B.
C. things that are boring
D.

Look. I've made it easy for you. This is why people like me.

For a Tudor, boredom is our weakness, our Kryptonite, our Achilles heel, that one missing scale in the dragon's body armour that brings down the dragon in every movie ever made about bringing down dragons.

As long as you avoid being bored, all is well. Forget this to your peril – you'll see why in Chapter 36.

DO NOT CHEAT BY SKIPPING FORWARD!

Chapter 6
The First of Rather a Lot of Chapters About Love

Tudor Love Tip: Listen to her. Hold her hand. Make her feel like she's the only womb in the world.

As you've probably already guessed, sweet book-buying person, I am in love with love. Yes, I've been married six times and have enjoyed many a sweet afternoon (evening, mid-morning, pre- and post-breakfast, etc.) with sundry mistresses. This is well known. But please also recall that 'twas I who popularised St. Valentine's Day as a celebration of hearts, flowers, cuddles, and kisses.

My very soul is supercharged with the lightning crackle of *amour*. I spend my day positively splashing about in the poetry of romance. When not violently putting down a rebellion in the North, plundering bits of France, or having heretics burnt at Smithfield, I am likely sighing at my window thinking of a lady beloved. Or perhaps I'm doing all of the above. I do multitask, you know. (Not long ago I noticed that your BBC4 was showing a film called *Henry VIII: Patron or Plunderer?* Srsly? I am beyond capable of managing both and then some simultaneously. The more accurate title would be *Henry VIII: Patron And Plunderer And Padded Poet And Pale Painstaking Paramour and Pilfering Pedantic Polyglot And Passionate Alliteration Appreciator.*)

Let me be perfectly clear, and this gets to the very purpose of this book, I know what a healthy, balanced, mindful life is – and especially know what love is – in spite of all the chatter to the contrary just now (more on this later). Look, if I didn't know love down to its lacy bits, please explain how I could write sensuous and meaningful verse such as:

> There once was a girl named Boleyn,
> Whose knickers I wisht to be in,
> But after we wed
> She cheated my bed
> And I divorced her neck from her chin.

That's a really good one. Here's another, its equal or better:

> I'm Henricus Rex
> And have regular sex
> As I'm in want of an heir.
> I'm sexy & cute
> When I play my lute
> And dance without clothes or care.

Every time I read that one I hear the sounds of cheering and applause in my head.

So, yes, I have seen love from one side to the other; I have measured its depths; I know love from its luscious lips to its squeeze-y bum. And through this book I intend to fully prove this to the satisfaction of all those who shall eventually be named. (Be patient, more on this later. It involves sex and the after-life; you'll like it.)

What we have learned in Chapter 6

- Hard to believe this is Chapter 6 already, where does the time go?

- Poems make love happen especially when you're naked

- There's nothing wrong and everything right with cheering and applause in your head

Chapter 7
Shall We Dance?

Tudor Love Tip: Strum your lute sexily whilst performing an alluring galliard in your underpants, then join her in bed with a shout of "IT'S GO TIME!"

It's tempting to envy a dog. All he is given to do is eat, sleep, run a tongue about his rude bits, play sniffy-the-arse with other canines, slink about devouring lumps of crunchy cat shit and so on. To make dog-heirs, he has a quick, ridiculous hump out in the street at midday. With no more ceremony than a yawn he's completed his dynastic obligations – pups on the way and a new generation gamboling in to replace the previous.

For men and women, however, in our calamitous semi-divine state, located somewhere on the Great Chain of Being between angels' wings and monkeys' bums, we require something golden and fantastical to go along with our rumpity-pumpity.

Love.

Love the trickster.

Love the complicator.

Love the battlefield.

We cannot simply shag on a whim outside the wheelwright's shop. No, no. We must write verse. We must learn to arrange our hair, remember how to hold our elbows at table, wear proper shoes, adjust hats at an ain't-I-something-special angle, learn the names of French wine regions, feign gaiety, and smile and/or scowl when we think it will be of benefit to our careers in romance. We yearn without admitting it, long whilst concealing our longing, and burn inwardly to run whilst we place one foot in front of the other with the speed of January ice melting. Oh, and many of you dance quite badly whilst believing otherwise.

Such a mystery it is. I remember as a boy my mum and I were once on a boat gliding along the Thames on one of those spring afternoons when the season is preparing to give itself away to summer. Her eyes were closed and her long white Plantagenet fingers were trailing languorously in the water. And I asked her, "Mummy, what is love exactly? Is it a feeling in your heart?"

She didn't answer right away and so I pressed my question.

"Is love a feeling one has in one's heart, Mummy?"

"Yes," she answered gently without opening her eyes. "Naturally."

"Is it from God?" I asked. "Bishop Fisher says all good things are from God and so I was wondering if you thought that was so too. Granny Beaufort puts ever so much stock in every word from Fisher's mouth, you know. So. Is love from God? Is it from God, Mummy? Is it, do you suppose?"

"Oh yes, Henry. Yes, yes. Why not?"

"Is it a kiss?"

"Quite."

"Is it that moment when you can't decide which of two men you shall be married to and then one man, we'll call him Henry VII, mercilessly slaughters the other, we'll give him the name Richard III, at Bosworth Field and then buries him in a car park?"

She smiled serenely. "I should think so."

21

"How can love be so many things, Mummy?"

Then she opened one eye. "Be a dear and see about one of the boatmen getting your darling Mum some more wine."

"Erm. Yes but we were talking about love."

"We were? Oh yes. Lovely that. Just lovely, dear. So now you know. Sorted. Ah, here comes that wine."

Later I asked her, growing suspicious, if love was a sack of boiled hedgehogs and she replied that she was sleepy and couldn't be arsed.

All of which is to say that I have done you the favour – by writing this book – that my own mother could not, or would not, do for me: reveal for all time the secrets of relationships, love, and romance. For you see all of the other bits – leadership, learning to manage your moods, parenting, marriage, divorce, embracing obesity, making history, managing your death and afterlife – *unleashing your inner Tudor* – all of it begins with love in its many forms and disguises and radiates outward.

So whether you're a girl of 14 about to be married to a duke five times your age, a young turk striding through court like a colossus wondering why your codpiece isn't attracting the attention it deserves, a dowager in her 70s hoping to spark the fancy of the shy gardener taking a casual piss in your climbing roses, this business of attraction and ardor is filled with heaps and heaps of bollocks. And yet, it is the centre. It is tricky, treacherous, and slippy-slide-y. The realm of love is a place where the kindest act, the purest moment, the most innocent motive can have galling ripple effects and ill winds.

In Chapter 8 I shall give you the best possible example of what I mean.

What We Have Learnt in Chapter 7:
- Whilst dogs are hairy imbeciles, they may not be wrong
- Love is what you're stuck with when you finally get round to reading the contract you signed with Lust
- Bad dancing
- Wine is the engine of motherhood

Your Tudor Weekly Plan

To *Unleash Your Inner Tudor* one really has got to master the complex balance between violent spontaneity and the careful planned manoeuvre, or more simply put, finding the sweet spot between screaming and scheming. Throughout this book I shall give you the tools for both. Here is the planned-out bit. You absolutely must begin each day with a to-do list. This will keep you on task whilst at the same time allowing you to riff as sociopathically as needed.

Sunday: (For those who have started their own church)
- Prayers
- Holy bread
- Holy wine
- Affix holy expression to face
- Wholly impregnate a lady
- Feel the glory/be the glory
- More holy wine
- Beef

Chapter 8
When the Moon Hits Your Eye Like a Big Fornication Pie

Tudor Love Tip: When a lady hurls her under-things to the floor and leaps upon your person, save all discussion of favourite hobbies for another time.

Greenwich Palace, 1506. When I was 15 years old, an older lady (late 20s, I think) appeared one afternoon in my rooms letting me know that she'd been sent round by England's Privy Council to "show me the ropes". (The Privy Council was made of my dad's glowering, furry-eyebrowed, dodgy friends who ran the country.) Apparently these were to be girly, coquettish ropes because she flounced about me like a colt with large, insinuating eyes. This pleased me for I had made a study of knots, loops, and coils and was delighted to show this goodly, Christian lady all that I knew and was eager to learn all that I could of her.

I was a fan especial of the savoy knot, also called the Flemish knot or the figure-eight and was readying myself to show this to her when I came in for a shock. Without preamble her fantastic lady pomegranates sprang from her bodice and the next thing I knew, with a frantic untying of laces and stays, my world became all armpits and elbows and a thatch of dark pubic hair (hers) against an egg-shell coloured torso, a wobbly tum with an odd inny-outy navel all of which was flummoxing away atop me like a canoe filled with badgers in a bouncy castle.

Next thing I knew something like an angel choir began to sing rather alarmingly and then exploded in my heir-making bits. A moment of panic – for I felt exactly as if important parts of me were flying off and soaring at tremendous speed across the room. Indeed some kind of ballast was torn away and I felt myself swirling up, up, upward out of a dark ocean that I did not know I had lived in all this time and was borne into the heavens where I was transformed into a glorious white cloud on a summer's day. And in that instant, the instant in which I wished to curl up in the puffy goodness of the universe and feel the immensity of love that had welled up inside of me, all the elbows and lovely white thighs and the glorious wobbly squishy bits were gone and my dad, Henry VII, stepped into the room and looking vapid, sallow, and awkward announced, "Henry VIII, my boy, this is what England requires of you."

"You're joking," I said, still trying to get my breath. "This –? Wait – with *ladies*?"

"Yes, of course," he said importantly.

"A lot?"

He gave me a firm nod meaning yes, loads.

OMG. I began to see my future as a very, very, very, very bright thing.

If the story ended there, it would be enchanting and uncomplicated – except for the Dad-appearing-unexpectedly part, which was weird and unsexy – but of course romantic episodes like this do not end where they ought because this is where people, sex, desire, and political necessity all intersect at a traffic circle called the Now You're Completely Fucked Memorial Roundabout.

The lady, whom I later enjoyed a few more all-nude-and-bonks with, turned out to be Elizabeth Boleyn, wife of courtier and ambassador Thomas Boleyn, a generous soul who minded not one whit that I was besmirching his wife in new and exhilarating ways, which made the Boleyns, in my mind, the apotheosis of all things stylish. This sophisticated power couple went on to produce three children, George, Mary, and Anne. And it is well known that I fathered none of them. And because it is well known, it is fact. Thus making what happened later betwixt Mary, Anne, and I not in the least bit pervy. Also, the whole thing was officially hushed up (to the point that historians get stroppy at the mention of it and will unfollow you on Twitter if you ever bring it up), so this is just between us.

What We Have Learnt in Chapter 8:
- Dads can be super weird
- If you can work it out to become king, or even the next in line, absolutely do it because ladies will fly out at you from all directions, rude bits aquiver and it's your job to bring your kingdom happiness in this way
- There's an angel choir in your underpants ready to sing, RIGHT NOW

Chapter 9
The Art of Wooing a Lady

Tudor Love Tip: Tell her that her smile makes your
codpiece suddenly far too small.

Whilst my experience with Elizabeth Boleyn
primed things for my heir-making duties – which
part goes where and in which order, etc. – they did
not prepare me in the least for the quixotic
mysteries that would come next – the wooing of a
lady.

Not that I needed to, really. As royals we
have our marriages fully arranged. The only action
required of us in the love and slapping-our-bacon-
together department are elective bits such as the
acquiring of mistresses. The getting of a wife is like
breakfast. It is handed to us and we enjoy it. I had
no more need of wooing a wife than I had of writing
sensual poetry to a boiled egg.

I, however, was unlike every royal who'd
come before. I was a new era. I was the pure,
glorious sunlight of the dawn of the Renaissance; I
was not a smelly, stringy-haired Mediaeval person
content with salted meat, mystery plays, hair shirts,
and no forks. Nay. I was a new man of red blood
and raw bone with the soul of a poet and a warrior.

To give romantic chase is as necessary as a
joust, a hunt, or the composition of verse.

To woo is the first step in the scintillating
journey that is love.

It's the first cha in the cha-cha-cha of
madness that is the mating dance. Birds do it, bees
do it, even Kathryn Howards on their knees do it.
(VILE TART!)

Winning the heart and other sporting bits of a lady is, of course, a subtle, skilled art, which begins by making sure she notices your codpiece.

I recommend selecting one with versatility. It bulges hugely at the base of your doublet, yes, but in a manner that says, "I'm as big as a horse but I'm not emotionally needy *like* a horse." You know how horses are – always wishing to be trotted about gently and spoken to in a just-so sort of voice calibrated not to spook and fed an apple every time they aren't crushed under your weight.

When you've got the size right with the proper mix of jewels, velvet, cloth of gold and silver tassels – and this can take any number of fittings – then you want a codpiece that can work with the mood of the moment. Sometimes I attach googly eyes on the end of mine and give it a wiggle pretending as though there's a little Jonah with a high falsetto voice inside who's been swallowed whole by a great whale. At other times I want it to shoot a fountain of sparkly flames. When the moment is right. Like at an intimate supper just before the cheese course.

Once she sees that you are serious about the housing and advertising of your brilliant dynasty-making wares, she will see you as a gentleman of consequence. And as Pepin the Short once wrote, "Confidence is sexy."

Next – and I hope you're taking good notes – it is time for poetry. Ladies love to tart things up with verse, especially the sort that celebrates ladies in all their glorious ladyness. Here's a good example in which I praise my sweet beloved for her many fine qualities and invite her to become part of English history:

I like your hair,
I like your pair,
Let's make an heir.

You see, it doesn't have to be complicated. Here's
one that Anne Boleyn quite liked.

Roses are red,
Violets are blue,
I should like to make
Hot, sweet love to you.
(Or your sister. I could go either
way.)

In retrospect I'm not positive she liked it-
liked it. She was constantly scowling about one
thing or another so it wasn't always easy to tell.
Oftimes a lady revels in you making
reference to your feelings about other ladies in your
life, specifically, those who came before her.
Catherine Parr quite liked this one about various
exes:

Roses are red,
Violets are blue,
I'm still glad
I beheaded you.

Here's one about Kathryn Howard:

There once was a girl with a rump,
That liked to go humpity-bump,
But after we wed
She cheated my bed
And now her nice neck is a stump.

And anytime you can intertwine food
and love, it's always going to be a big hit,
like this one:

> She's achin' for my bacon
> Begs for my eggs
> Makes a hostage
> Of my saustage
> Sex breakfast!

Of course Rule One in the art of erotic
poetry is "never be predictable," always the first
step toward mediocrity. As such I have written quite
a lot of modern, sexy, non-rhyming verse. Here's a
miscellany:

> Are you quite ready,
> I whisper,
> to have greatness thrust upon you?

> ***

> The fire crackles,
> I strum my lute sexily
> With my shirt open,
> Whilst your lips part,
> I eat a mallard.

> ***

> Reds are red
> Violets are blue
> Have you noticed my codpiece?
> Boobs.

***

That's not a unicorn
In my pocket
Greensleeves!

What comes next is obvious. You need smoking-hot dance moves. If I can ever get one of these bloody time travelers who plagues my court to bring a video camera, I shall be pleased to demonstrate some of my more seductive dance-floor-destroying manoeuvres. Until then, you'll just have to remember:

A) Start slow making her think you're all gravitas and stateliness

B) Work to a sharper rhythm

C) Put on a show of alarming sexiness. And I do mean <u>alarming</u> – taking her to the brink where she doesn't know if you're going to gloriously trombone her in the antechamber or maim her with a spade. And for a moment, maybe you don't either. All that matters is the dance – the sizzling, barbaric sensation that is detonating in your trousers.

Finally you'll need palaces, land, servants, plate, jewels, beds that are free of lice (mostly), a title, and a private army. All of these are, for your intended, the outward signs of the sort of man you are.

If you have none of the above, you may simply need to invite her over, uncork a couple bottles of wine, take off your shirt, strike sexy poses, and hope for the best.

What We've Learnt in Chapter 9:

- Make your codpiece work for you – one that says 'I'm all man in the head and all Centaur in the undercrackers'

- Erotic poetry oils the chute to pumping your party bits together

- Sexy dance moves. Need I say more? I probably do but we'll move on.

Your Tudor Weekly Plan

Monday:
- lie-in
- create reality in which it is not Monday and I am crowned King of France
- shout irrational thoughts
- nap

Chapter 10
On Wooing a Gentleman

*Tudor Love Tip: The man of your dreams is only
one crazy-hot act of seduction away even if you're
on a train or buying groceries*

Ladies, you, of course, have an unfair advantage in the wooing business. Your mysterious ways, your indefinable radiances, your hotness, your allure. It's almost too easy.

Here's an example of just how simple it is for you. Once whilst hunting in a royal forest I dismounted and stopped to water an alder when a lovely shepherdess emerged from a hedge nearby and called out cheerfully, "Fancy a shag, your highness?" To which a man's answer WILL *ALWAYS* BE YES. Even if he is coughing up bile on his deathbed with a lance sticking straight through his face he will take you up on this fantastic offer.

But I understand well that ladies wish to be more intriguing and needlessly complicated about it. They wish to dress exquisitely and have some music on, with a few candles to set the stage. I can offer you guidance here as well of course.

Imagine you're at a dance at a great hall, we'll say it's Greenwich Palace. Firelight plays amongst the huge oaken beams and illumines the vast tapestries of mythological and biblical imagery. There are the sounds of harp, fife, lute, and drum set to the music of the rustle of dresses of silk and damask and cloth of gold. Tables are laden with meats and delicate cheeses and hearty wines, festooning the air with the incense of savoury and sweet.

You are dancing a galliard with a gentleman whom you quite fancy. But you do not simply dance. No, no. You do not simply make coltish advances with your eyes. If you are serious about this gentleman, you pull him aside, into a half-lit alcove, and you take his hand in yours. You lock eyes and you slide his hand inside the upper rim of your bodice across the smooth, rounded, hot, thick gorgeousness of one of your lady montañas. I must insist that you confine this move to one breast. (Write this down!) If you are indecisive, thinking, "No, this one. Wait, no really this is the better one. No, no back to the one before," whisking his hand quickly back and forth, back and forth, between the two, it spoils the mood a bit, moving into Punch-and-Judy territory. Likewise if you take both of his hands and slide them palm-facing into the upper reach of your dress, there's a great deal of physical awkwardness especially if you are determined to keep his palms on your upsurge of ladiness, thus running the risk of breaking his elbows. I've seen this go badly.

My point is – you, darling – taking the initiative in this startling manner, whilst maintaining cool eye contact, lips parted, your moist tongue, like a damp candy just at the gateway of your youthful mouth – ow, crikey! My codpiece is suddenly much too tight. Oh bugger. Oooff that stings. [Edit this bit out later.]

He's yours. In that instant. Yours. No matter how loudly his wife may be shrieking at him. The only person in the world at that moment is you.

That's really, truly and completely all it requires.

Why more ladies don't do this is a puzzle. Perhaps they're looking for something more dramatic, more in the realm of gamesmanship or statecraft. Such a pointless waste of time.

Later we will discuss the definitive ways to keep your man once you've sunk your love-talons into him.

What We've Learnt in Chapter 10:
- Wooing for men = codpiece, sexy dance moves, poetry, land, money, private army, castles, title
- Wooing for ladies = boobs

Chapter 11
When One Has the Misfortune to Receive Crap Lessons in Leadership from One's Own Dad

Tudor Leadership Tip: The true leader re-writes history the way a hammer re-writes a stained-glass window.

We'll get to the practical application of wooing in the next chapter but for now we delve into the secrets of leadership – though, keep in mind, here too there are lots of sexy bits so prepare to be made frightfully aroused. Loose clothing, I should think. A comfortable chair. Send the children out of the room. Have a servant fan you with ostrich feathers.

We are backing up a bit to the glorious year 1501, when I first beheld the woman who one day would be my first wife, Catherine of Aragon. In typical romcom style, I met her at a wedding – hers, as it turns out. She was becoming married to my older brother, Arthur. And, Sweet Christ on a unicorn, I knew I must have her. I knew I must be the summer wind in her wheat, the moonlight glittering upon her ocean, the thoughts of folly in her wine.

There were, however, more barriers to this goal than were ever faced by Hobbits tossing jewelry into volcanoes. Beginning with the fact that I was not next in line to the throne and therefore, naturally, less interesting to her. As first-born male baby person in our family, Arthur was to be king. It was he who trotted about with Dad learning how one extracts money from the nobility, how to sit on a horse and gaze gravely and serenely across a field while the breeze moves gently through your hair and men await your command, and how to look magnificent on a throne that may or may not be legitimately yours. It was he who was secretly and carefully schooled in the arts of leadership.

Meanwhile I frolicked meaninglessly at Greenwich Palace with my mum and my sisters, Margaret and Mary, and was intended to grow up and do a lot of jousting, fornicating, feasting, dancing, winning of poetry contests, and being generally incredible. I was the understudy no one ever expected to need.

Not a bad life but not the elevated position that I saw for myself.

What I'm trying to convey is that you gotta have a dream. When you give up your dream, you die. For those of you keeping track, I said that 500 years before it was in *Flashdance*.

But like it or not, Arthur was the heir. I, the spare.

He was the one who would go down in the history books, lead men into battle, sit on the glittery throne of England and sire the next king. He was the one BBC2 would lather on about. Meanwhile, I'd be offered some poncey church job where my highest aspiration in life would be to go about in a floppy red Cardinal's hat from sodding Rome.

Not enough glory to dip your balls in.

No one writes history books about the boy who comes in second. Or if they do they become the sort that ends up on that pitiful wheeled cart that sits on the street just outside the bookshop with a "70% discount" sign getting rained upon. Poor Dan Snow is left to try to wheeze some life into them on his history podcast.

Late one summer afternoon when I was about five or six years old I tracked the movements of my father, the king, until I spied him seated in the garden at Whitehall plotting ways of fattening the treasury with his revolting, doddery old friends Edmund Dudley and Sir Richard Empson. After his cronies hurried off to do their various oily deeds, I found the courage to approach. Dad did not often encounter people my size and seemed surprised when I greeted him, as though I were a talking goat.

"Your Grace," I said with a bow.

"Greetings, miniscule person," he said, a bit unclear on whom I was or why I was there before him.

"It is I, your son," I said in a clarifying sort of way.

He chuckled. "You're not Arthur."

"I'm Henry," I said.

"Oh yes, Henry. That's right. Henry, yes, yes. Quite."

I put my question to him. "I should like to know, father, the secrets of being a great leader."

"Ah that," he said. "Well, I'm sure you're not plotting against me just yet are you?"

"Of course not," I replied. "I have only the greatest love for you, father."

"Good."

"I should like to learn from you the secrets of being a majestic and wise ruler."

"You do realise that you're not going to become a ruler, my child," said Henry VII. "Your job as the second son will be to become a leading light in the church and to never be with a lady or have children, while at the same time not being a homosexual, but instead to be fully devoted to

goodly and Godly things. You'll get a very nice hat.
Has anyone mentioned that?"

"Yes," I answered. "But I have an interest in
the qualities of a great leader. Surely even men of
the church require such knowledge."

Zing! I'd got him there.

"I see. Well," he said, with an over-dramatic
sigh. "It's complicated, obviously. It's, erm, that is,
there are countless, you know, important things,
kingly things which – Christ it's hot enough out
here to boil the tits off a camel. You know, one of
those great, hairy, humped beasts, they have in –"

"I know what a camel is. Unless of course
by humped beast you meant Richard III?" I said,
with a wry smile.

"No I meant a camel," he said with no trace
of humour. "Oh, look, there's Arthur!"

And so it was. Speaking of galumphing
creatures here was Arthur interrupting my colloquy
with father, appearing through the hydrangeas
dressed in a light summer robe with a garland of
flowers in his long, silly hair.

"Arthur!" father called out rapturously.
"Give him a bow, erm, boy," Dad said with a glance
at me. "Might as well get in the habit."

I bowed and muttered, "Die foul ooze."

The two of them went off taking great and
important joy in each other's company and I was
left to the buzzing of bees and the sound of
hedgehogs rutting in the roses.

The knife was given a very painful twist and
wiggle when a few years later Arthur got to marry
Catherine of Aragon, who was a SMOKING HOT
piece of girlhood who I thought was from
somewhere like France or Germany. Maybe Brazil.
I wasn't sure at the time, I simply knew she was

foreign. She was a bosomy, buxomy bit of yum with a little lisp and a lovely neck and various places on her body that were clearly made BY GOD HIMSELF for my kisses and caresses. And the flesh of my flesh and the bone of my bone. So it was difficult to watch that tattered dishcloth, my older brother, stand at St. Paul's and promise the entire kingdom that he would mercilessly hammer this lovely flower with his wangy-parts until she could withstand no more. Which was not bloody likely. Arthur was such a twat he could barely manage a Christmas-time wank. If you can't knock one out for Jesus on his birthday then you're not much arsing good in my book. Which you are fortunate to be reading.

After Arthur spent his first matrimonial eve with Catherine, he lustily announced that he'd "spent all night in Spain". Get it? She was from Spain. He was "in" Spain. FFS. Well, apparently foreign travel didn't agree with him because a mere four weeks later Arthur was dead.

Which is the all the proof needed that God likes me best.

But I wasn't king, not yet. No, Dad was still doing his gloomy, hollow-cheeked, morose impersonation of kinghood, raising people's taxes, not financing Christopher Columbus's New World expedition (not joking about this), sloping around the castle all pink and watery like an under-boiled chicken.

In fact, the morning of Arthur's funeral, Dad appeared in my room and handed me a letter, which would shape the remainder of my life – all my relationships and philosophy of leadership. It began:

~~My dearest first born Arthur~~ Henry,

As you approach the august date of your coronation, which will surely take place in the not-distant future, here is the list of things you must do for England:

1. Male heirs (more than one, VERY important!!! <u>Must</u>, <u>Must</u>, <u>MUST</u>!!!)
2. Keep England from civil war
3. Get/stay rich
4. Invade/conquer France (that throne is ours!!)
5. Tell Spain to piss actually off
6. Traumatise/destabilise Parliament & nobility on reg basis
7. Male heirs
8. Male heirs
9. Male heirs
10. <u>Male</u> bloody <u>heirs</u>
11. #StayInspired

After giving this list a glance, I said it looked fine. No problem. Consider it done. Sorted.

Dad seemed put off by my nonchalance – cheeks went a bit red.

"Ah youth," he said in a passive-aggressive sort of way.

"What?!" I demanded.

"Boy, you have so much to learn about leadership," he growled.

"My name is Henry."

"Whoever you are. You don't know even the basics of being a ruler. And you seem to resist all I have to teach you."

"You've never tried to teach me anything," I responded icily, landing what I considered to be a stunning blow.

43

I waited for these words to take their effect.

I had been very icy.

I imagined him crumpling to the floor, looking up at me, his very soul impaled by the sharp truth of my words, his eyes large, damp, and frightened.

But he did none of those things.

He simply drew in a breath and his eyes took on that fire they always did when he was about to say something of supreme importance.

"Fake it until you make it," he intoned solemnly.

"Really?"

"Yes."

"Anything else?"

"Being King is the Thing," he added.

"OK."

He eyed me sternly. "Find a way to make them pay."

"Does all your leadership advice rhyme?" I asked.

"It's a mnemonic device. Helps you remember it."

"Oh my God, Dad, it's the 16th Century. You do know we have quills, ink, and vellum? These days we can write shit down."

He raised his voice, "Let the nobles grab you not by the globbels!"

"That's not even a word!"

It was at that point he gave me an evil yet righteous glare and marched from the room. What a numpty – but truly, how hard could any of this stuff be?

Make a male heir? Pfft. Any peasant could do that. A dog can accomplish that one.

There were more immediate matters. I was a kid with the hots for my dead brother's fit, lovely, and newly single wife.

What We Have Learnt in Chapter 11
- Future leader, let your dreams soar like a great bird that reaches the highest heights and shits on whomever it pleases
- Your to-do list may be the tiniest bit harder than you suspect
- Think twice before rhyming advice

Your Tudor Weekly Plan

Tuesday:
- Eat
- Drink
- Shag
- Repeat

Chapter 12
The Practical Application of Wooing with Catherine of Aragon

Tudor Love Tip: Don't simply think of her as someone you'd like to shag. Think of her as – wait. Actually do think of her simply as someone you'd like to shag, it could well be the only happiness you'll ever get.

From leadership back to wooing. Keep up.

I begged Holbein to produce a painting of what Catherine of Aragon might look like emerging from a mythological bathing pool on a cold morning. Nearly naked!

And not too cold, mind, but cold enough. RAWR!

Holbein agreed to produce something on a smaller scale, a miniature of one of her duckies. Which he did (from his imagination? From real life? I'd never thought about it until just now) and I had it framed in lovely gilt edged with emeralds. I smuggled this image about in my gowns, sneaking bawdy glances and nearly weeping in ecstasy.

This is how things go in royal households. No one gets to tell us what to do, so there's loads of rude painting and unseemly prancing about between bedrooms, the writing of terrible erotic verse and poisoning and the purchasing of expensive capes; there's screaming and scheming for power and nipple slapping and ball tickling and what have you.

Keep in mind the Romans were far worse than we and the Merovingians were so shockingly deranged and depraved they made the Roman nobility look like sugar-dusted chipmunks in a magical land of pudding fairies.

But back to me gazing with intense longing at boob-portraits of Cat.

I was 11 when Arthur floated off to be with Jesus. Catalina (as she was sexily known in her native land) was 16. This is an age when five years can make a difference. Whilst I was now in line to become the king (and thus more intriguing than ever to girls and ladies and their scheming noble families everywhere), I was not yet old enough to consummate a marriage – or so it was popularly believed though I'm certain, given my prodigious gifts, I could have resplendently and successfully plundered Spain and sired any number of heirs on the spot.

My father, in true form, dithered over setting up a marriage contract with Catherine's father, the somebody-somebody of some minor caliphate in Spain. Dad wanted more money, the Spaniard dad in Spain arsed about in response. And Catherine, whilst kind and good and going about like sunlight, clearly saw me as a child and not yet as her future lord and master.

I knew that if The Little Princess of All-That was to be mine, I needed a plan.

First I would sully Arthur's memory, thus wounding her, making her feel vulnerable and emotionally needy and as such opening the door to her affections. (Are you taking this down?)

I located a copy of Arthur's personal Bible and on an inside page I sketched a hideous naked lady with powerful pointy tits and wrote "Catherine of A." and drew an arrow to her head and then scrawled the word "Bagina" and drew an arrow to her furry naughty business. I then solemnly approached Catherine and gave the holy book as a gift that I knew she would want to have. A tear hung in my eye.

She kissed the air near enough to my cheek that I felt the dizzying heat of her white, lightly freckled skin. I watched as she clutched the scriptures to her bosom and walked to a window where she began to leaf through it and saw her redden, her mouth tighten, and she choked a little bit.

Boom-shocka-locka.

Next I began a Cute Pet Names Campaign – quite useful. First I shortened Catalina to Cat. Then to:

Kitttens
Kit
Kit Cat
Kit Cat Shitbat
Kit Cat Gonna Hit Me Summa Dat
Feline
Fee
Fee-Fee Pee-Pee
Fee-Fi-Fo Who My Little Ho
Spanish Inquisition
Etc.

And I promise you, out of sheer frolic, I once called her That Bit Of Tail I'm Going To So Throw Over If She Doesn't Pump Out A Boy Child. I was completely joking. I mean, who knew?

With time, I did feel Catherine begin to succumb to the inevitable. Besides my obvious physical charms, my horsemanship, my falconry, my incredible singing voice, my extremely fine calf, etc., she at last became mine when my father began to entertain thoughts of marrying her himself,

49

smiling at her with bits of pork in his crooked teeth at supper. Quite a show for a monarch who normally did a stunning impression of a winter vegetable just pulled from a summer drain. The idea of Dad marrying Catherine himself was horrifying, a real wake-up call to her and, really, to all of Christendom. Arrangement or no at some point she'd have to see him naked – all white and veiny and slack – and then work up the nerve to play horsey-and-rider.

Eventually good taste began to have its effect and after ceaseless negotiations it began to look as though Catherine and I might marry. But the bargain was not yet done.

What We Have Learnt in Chapter 12:
- If you want your dead brother's wife, have a plan
- Boob portraits
- Cute names
- Your dad's repellent display of old-man horn-doggery will drive her to you (USE THAT!)

Tudor Love Tips – Exercise
Gentlemen's List

Like the list of demands my dad gave me (mostly about making male heirs), you need a list as it gives structure and strategy to your relationships – mostly an illusion, but like so many illusions, useful and user-friendly.

Men's List
Gentleman reader, your list will be different than mine as God didn't choose you be to a superior person. But, given your status as a human with a scrotum, the general outline should include:
- Male heirs (obvs)
- Invade Scotland and/or adjacent dodgy nation
- Develop an iconic fashion look, like, really wide shoulders and hosiery of hotness
- Face minted on a coin
- Build ships
- Plunder properties owned by The Pope
- Showtime series about your life, which includes Natalie Dormer and loads of almost-real-looking bumpy-humpy.

Lady's List
Obviously as a lady person a list such as this must be made for you by your father or husband. Failing that it should be produced on your behalf by a brother, uncle, or nearest male relative, although if pressed it could be a banker, local tradesman, shepherd on a nearby hill, could even be a child who can write, or a skanky troll who lives under a

bridge and frightens storybook goats. The point is a man needs to create this list for you.

Here's what it should include:
- the production of male heirs
- a lifetime of needlework
- the wearing of hats
- looking nice in a portrait
- being cool about mistresses
- not shagging the servants
- loads of recreational bonkity-wonkity

Expand Your Relationship Vocabulary, Enlarge Your World

Kingle:
When you always seem to be a bit married and yet always a bit single, and you are king

Chapter 13
What Women Want

Tudor Love Tip: The First Step To Understanding Ladies Is Being Clear that What They Truly, Really, Completely Want is Something You Will Never Be Able to Give Them

Even less than halfway through this book it should be self-evident what women desire most. But for those of you who have not yet connected the dots, let us now enumerate the four things that women want (that's right precisely four):

1. They want me.
2. They want to be my queen.
3. They want to give glorious birth to my manly and aggressively masculine male offspring.
4. They want to luxuriate and flounce about at Hampton Court Palace, Greenwich, Whitehall, Nonsuch, etc. – to wear floaty dresses with Ladies-in-Waiting attending to their various feminine needs and whims and hygiene issues, musicians performing sweet and vaguely erotic songs for them, poets composing sonnets to their beauty, and foreign ambassadors uttering shite like "My Lady" and "Madam" in those contemptible accents.

Here's what ladies energetically do not want:
1. Men who are not me
Let's keep it real. Expecting a woman to sleep with you whilst not being me is a pretty big ask. But here's the good news: I cannot be in all places in all

times. And I don't think it's too personal to mention that I have but one codpiece, and one notorious MHDS housed within said codpiece – though talented and astonishing – to go around. So your advantage, modern male, is also that you're not me.

Ironic.

No matter how much the women of your era desire me, they cannot have me, except when they close their eyes, though I wish to Sweet Hippie Jesus this were not so. I am pinned down in time, unable to share the colossal gifts God hath given unto me and to me alone. This is the biggest, ugliest, most messed-up misfortune in the history of the universe.

Wait.

Wait …

Do you ever have that moment when you've written something so heartbreaking, so bleak, so massive that you put down your quill and suddenly feel as though your very soul has just been shattered …

That feeling of being the only one of your kind …

Imagine you were the only manticore (a mythological lion/dragon/scorpion/bat creature), who has a 52-inch waist, gout, diabetes and personality disorders … and then you got a Twitter account …

Wow. My eyes are watering.

Okay, moving on.

Trying to move on. The pain, ouch.

Okay. Deep breaths.

I have taken what some readers might see as a circuitous route to my point in this chapter. To which I would say LEARN YOUR PLACE WORM! Wait – that just comes out automatically.

What I meant to say is that the pathway to truth is not straight. I often find, for example, that the pathway to truth runs through the kitchen and then into the wine cellar, stopping off at the bath, and the bedchamber of one or two ladies of the court. But that's me.

Here's where this chapter has been headed this whole time. Take heed.

Whilst you cannot be me, modern man who wishes to attract a lady, you can be *like* me, which is as near as you can get. And you'll be doing her the enormous favour of almost making her dreams come true.

Read on and embrace the stars.

What We Have Learnt in Chapter 13:

- There are FOUR things women want and all of them have to do with being by my side. Or on top of me. Or under me. Depending on mood.

- The one thing women don't particularly care for is a man who is not me. You can be sad now.

- The simple way to remember all this is that ladies want what is out of reach and have no interest in that which is easily accessible

- Fat manticore

Chapter 14
The Art of the Marriage Deal

Tudor Love Tip: The cause of the downfall of your relationship is always sitting out in plain view ready to be recognised instantly in hindsight.

And so the deal remained infuriatingly undone – the marriage contract, which would have been arranged between Catherine and my delicious self. Our Dad's names were signed to various draft contracts. Impressive royal wax seals were affixed time and again. Documents flew back and forth from England to Spain in mere weeks. (The speed of 16th century communication is pretty exciting!) Old people can take an excruciatingly long time to make up their minds.

I was pretty certain Catherine was into the whole idea too. She didn't say so outright but I know things. Lady things.

I was sure that as far as the ruling classes in the two countries were concerned it would be a win that went both ways. The Tudors would officially and completely bonk their way into the European royalty club and Dad would get a lovely sum of money. Eventually. Probably. And Aragon got an ally in the never-ending struggle to make France explode.

What was less known (or given a toss about) was that a marriage to Catherine would be a win for me too. I desired her, which, of course, means I loved her, and that mattered to me, though that sort of thing was not supposed to rank terribly high.

The list of things a royal son was asked to care about in his wife-to-be began with:

1. Capable of producing male heirs

2. Brings shit-ton of money into treasury/family coffers via dowry

3. Creates alliance with her Dad, who is now less likely to invade, burn, pillage, stab, break things, etc.

4. Perpetuates a class system (created by God) which works out nicely for our fam

Somewhere in the 40s or 50s on such a list – down past "Not a Witch" and "Has Correct Number of Nipples" – would be "in love with her" and "Sweet Jehovah she looks good".

I adored Catherine's voice, her inviting eyes, the curve of her hand on a bannister, which I could imagine would be the same angle as when she held my hand one day. I could not wait to undress her, following the lines of stays and buttons and ties in her gowns and under-gowns and under-under-gowns like little feet printed on a treasure map all the way to splendor.

There was this one tiny spot of bother. A faint voice of warning in the back of my head saying, "But she was once rammed and boarded by your brother ..."

But then there was another booming voice that said, "Arthur was such a nimrod he probably never really worked himself up to plundering Spain. At least not much. LOL."

OK statistically speaking it was possible that Arthur had managed a jump-and-thump with Catherine, in the same way that it's theoretically possible for an albatross to build an aqueduct.

And really what could it possibly matter?

Yes, there is that verse in that Holy Bible, Leviticus 20:21, that says, "And if a man shall take his brother's wife, it is an unclean thing: he hath uncovered his brother's nakedness; they shall be childless."

Haha. Did that really apply in this situation? It was probably just meant for peasants or Jews, right? I put the question to several theologians and biblical scholars, who said that yes in fact it did apply, which I found extremely rude and traitorous, since it was not the answer I was looking for.

Dad sent the Pope some nice sparkly gifts and the Pope then said we were cool. Everything would be fine on the Jehovah front. My beautiful marriage would not be cursed by God or anything. What could go wrong? And yet forces in England and Spain conspired against us.

What We Have Learnt in Chapter 14

- In the search for answers keep looking until you get the one you want

- Love is all you need once you've got everything else

- Go with the booming voice; it's the fun one

- Bribes

Expand Your Relationship Vocabulary, Enlarge Your World

Sister-in-RAWR!!:
When your brother's wife is smoking hot and you dream of the day the two of you shall make sweet and frequent rumpity-pumpity

Chapter 15
Removing Elderly Obstacles on Your Path to Glory

Tudor Leadership Tip: Your True Leadership Potential Will Never Soar Like Eagles With an Old Lady All Up In Your Grill

With my brother Arthur dead and Dad not looking terribly healthy, there was only one other person standing between me and ultimate power in the land. That was my grandmother.

Margaret Beaufort was as tiny as one of your canisters of pepper spray and just as alarming. She'd been married, on the order of Henry VI, to the dashing and handsome 24-year-old Edmund Tudor in 1444-ish. She was 12 when they wed. I'm sure she made a lovely bride. She celebrated becoming a teenager the following year by giving birth to my dad. I know what you're thinking, modern person, and I command you to stop. There shall be no retching noises whilst the covers of this book are open! Obviously God wished things to go this way so it's all entirely normal and non-creepy. If God didn't want child brides they wouldn't exists – JUST LIKE ZEBRAS!

My Gran lived through a lot of scary and horrible things – she was married four times, for example. Oh and she survived, if not thrived during the Wars of the Roses. And as the saying goes, what doesn't kill you makes you pushy and unlikeable. When Dad became king he was always a little afraid of Gran and to placate her (an impossible task) gave her a fancy title, the authority to dole out justice in the north (to get her as far away as possible), and the ability to own land as though she were a man. Once at dinner when her tiny person was hurling rather a lot of abuse and invective at him I heard him mutter the name Margaret Blow Forth. So yes Dad had the throne but she had Dad, so to speak.

In royal families death is the thing everyone waits about for. Dad was, I'm sure, waiting for Gran to snuff it and let him enjoy his kingship unencumbered. I was waiting for Dad to croak so I could take the throne. The trick involved in waiting for a parent to die is to not look too yearning about it. Dad knew I was waiting for it. I knew he knew I was waiting for it. But we were both waiting for Gran to go tits up so it brought us together.

Surely it couldn't take much longer as she was about 8,000 years old; I felt all the pieces of the puzzle locking into place.

On the morning of 21 April 1509 I heard shouts from down the gallery about someone being dead and I raised my voice to God and I said, "Thank you dear Sweet Saviour for taking one for the team and allowing Gran to join you in heavenly splendour."

And that's when the old bat herself appeared in my door.

I lurched from her ghastly, wraith-like though fully non-dead figure.

She grinned horribly and said, "The king is dead. Long live the king!"

Dad was gone. Now I had the throne but alas with my grandmother still alive, so really as far as she was concerned, it was "throne" in air quotes and with quite a lot of sarcasm.

Shit.

"Praise be to God," we both said at the same time.

"I said it first," I muttered.

She was undeterred. "Henry, as your first act as king you must –"

"Execute Edmund Dudley and Sir Richard Empson!" we both shouted simultaneously.

"Bloody hell, I said it first, Gran. It was my bloody idea!"

"Through their machinations and cruelty Dudley and Empson have extracted vast sums of money from the nobility, merchant, and peasant classes and have made the crown extremely wealthy. However, they are hated by all the people. Only their blood will quell the restless populace and vaunt you to glory," she said providing the exposition that this chapter rather badly needed.

"I know what to do," I said. "I'm 17 years old!"

(In an era during which most people were dead by the age of 40 this sounded more impressive.)

She looked at me through her all-knowing eyes, which I'm pretty certain made her George Lucas's model for the Emperor in those Star Wars movies.

"Please go," I said, "I've got my coronation to plan."

"I've already done it," she said, unfurling a document.

"No you haven't!"

"Yes I have," she said as calm as a foundation stone. "Beyond that, you must of course marry – "

"Catherine of Aragon!" I growled. "I've already made up my mind to do so!"

"Then you're following my plan for you to the letter."

"It's not your plan, it's mine! It's been mine all along!"

"Whatever."

I glared at her. She give a detestable smirk of superiority.

"Be gone, old woman, I've got my wedding to plan!"

"I've done that too."

"No! You! Have! Sodding! Not! You have not planned my wedding!"

"Yes I have," she said.

"YOU'RE NOT THE BOSS OF ME!" I shouted in all-caps.

But her crinkly, ancient eyes told a rather different story.

Gran was always something of a planner. The worse things got the more she schemed.

A bit of background. There is a period of English history known in your era as The Wars of The Roses, but which I grew up thinking of as that 50-year stretch during which my grandparents and great-grandparents all stabbed each other a lot.

It became a bit like Romeo and Juliet, really. Two great houses with loads of brothers and cousins and manservants all eager to do each other in. In this case rather than the Capulets and the Montagues it was the Lancastrians (our side) and the Yorkists (think Richard III and then try not to vom). There were countless battles, schemes, plots, murders, runnings about and this and that king being set up and then deposed and then being chased about the countryside. My mother's family, the Plantagenets, were Yorkists, and Dad's family, the Tudors, were all Lancastrians.

To complete the Romeo and Juliet comparison, from these two great, warring houses came my mum and dad, who got married against all odds – though in the Lord's great mercy Phil Collins was not around at the time to sing about it – and instead of committing suicide they had quite a number of children.

And, yes, Gran had planned their wedding. For that matter, Gran placed herself in it, the old sea monster.

Lots of people accused dad of being a usurper and those people were killed. Dad was not the most creative person in the world but he was thorough. How he and Arthur used to love reviewing accounts and tax sheets and finding loopholes in treaties. OMG. If my dad had a genius for anything it was for making monarchy as boring as shit.

So now I was king. And dear old Gran was industriously and authoritatively planning my wedding. Without "checking in with her" I set about planning my wedding too.

First obviously I did what dad could not do. I finalized things with Catherine's dad. Announced that it had been my dad's dying wish I would marry her and all the fight went out of him. The deal was done.

Gran then presented me with plans for a big, public affair. So instead I ensured that Catherine and I were wed in a quiet, private ceremony in a pretty chapel.

Gran gave me a list of what I must do for my coronation. In turn I then handed her list to my Groom of the Stool who used it to wipe my lovely royal arse.

There was nothing that little package of explosives could do about it.

I had an army, spies, and henchmen. She had force of personality.

But unlike dad, I had force of personality too.

Check and mate.

The result was that everyone at court began to realise that indeed a new day had dawned and it was I, not Margaret Beaufort, who was large and in charge.

Within a few days of my coronation, she died. Not saying I killed her.

But I may have ignored her to death.

What we have learnt in chapter 15

- The path to leadership can be as simple as polishing your bum with strategically chosen documents
    - Often winning is simply shouting louder
    - Show your granny who's boss

Your Tudor Weekly Plan

Wednesday:
- Lazy day
- Maybe insult Spain
- Perhaps burn heretics
- Probably traumatise Parliament
- WILL make an heir
- Nap

Chapter 16
You Know that Period of Gloating When
You Get Married and Show The Rest of the World
How It's Done? Enjoy It Whilst You Can ...

*Tudor Love Tip: God gave us marriage that
we might more fully appreciate wine*

I was officially crowned 23 June at St.
Paul's, and enjoyed the day with my new bride.
Catherine and I rode side by side through the streets
that day with crowds cheering and tossing garlands
of roses, wine flowing in fountains throughout
London, the skies ablaze with light and when I
looked over at her, this woman, this divinity, I so
wanted to breathe but often found that I could not.

My marriage would be different than other
royal marriages. It would be perfect and special. It
would be about love, not simply alliances. My court
would be way better than my dad's – filled with
loads of scholars, poets, theologians, musicians,
composers, thinkers and dreamers. It was 1509, the
year all future generations would look back upon
and say, "Ah yes, that's when everything became
and stayed fantastic."

Amongst my first acts as king was indeed to
have Empson and Dudley, a couple of Dad's
friends, beheaded – good move. My idea. Everyone
loved me for that. You have to remember that this
was an era before the Internet, movies, the telly box,
strip clubs, or the English Premier League. People
were often bored shitless. When they could bring
the kids to a public burning, hanging,
disembowelment, or beheading it was like
Christmas. And when it was two famous and widely
disliked members of the nobility it was like

Christmas and *Britain's Got Talent* all rolled into one.

The next thing I did was to turn all the boring bits of government – fishing treaties, administration of lands, diplomacy – to a fellow named Cardinal Thomas Wolsey, who geeked-out on this sort of thing.

The being-king-bits that I personally held onto were:

- hunting
- archery
- jousting
- developing a wide stance
- booming laughter
- learning to do cool, scary things with my eyebrows
- growing a beard
- sword fighting
- mistresses
- invading France

In 1513 I did what any good king named Henry does, I personally led an invasion into France (looking at you V!). Whilst kicking arse at The Battle of the Spurs my brother-in-law James IV up in bloody Scotland thought it'd be good timing to lead an invasion into northern England. As I had buggered off across the English Channel, Catherine handled the Scots and at the Battle of Flodden James was killed and that was that. Beaten by a woman. Wow. How do you recover from that?

When I came home Catherine presented me with James's blood-soaked cloak and we high-fived. We were a winning team.

After that we did what any couple would do after butchering a lot of people, we had sex.

As one might imagine my superb marriage with Catherine went extremely well until it didn't.

What We Have Learnt in Chapter 16:
- Love is a kind of upper respiratory condition
- It's always healthy for a relationship when you both share a passion for having the same people killed
- Booming laughter

Chapter 17
For the Gentleman reader

Marriage – Mind-crippling Happiness is on its Way!

Alors. Gentlemen, it is my duty to report that God, who is completely brilliant in all ways, appears not to have devoted his full attention to the whole "making of ladies" business. Not saying there's anything wrong with that – no, no. The Lord Jehovah is a powerful, mighty, awesome deity in every regard and we all think he's fantastic. (I do hope he's reading this.) And the truth is he had plenty on his mind during creation week working out lands and seas, the sun, where to hide emeralds and diamonds from peasants, the mammals – sorting out their various flavours – making man from clay and so forth. Afterwards the Lord went on holiday – well deserved – and a few weeks later after drinks one night he said, "Oh I'll just throw in this last bit". And as a complete after-thought, he tossed together another man except this one had breasts, internal babymaking parts and a breathtaking sense of moral superiority. Suddenly all the things a man loves to do – hunting, fighting, pissing from high places onto lower places, drinking, gluttony, fart contests, stabbing things, and so on – came under every kind of disapproving scrutiny.

According to my sources, Adam complained about this "whoa-man" to God after our Lord and Maker had awoken the next day feeling unwell; Jehovah's response was then to immediately implant in Adam's mind the frenzied and unquenchable desire to have sex with Eve, thus

71

rendering her bearable and making it look like this had been God's idea all along.

To be fair, the Lord gave Eve the desire for having a romp too, but with a catch – her sex drive came with an odd sort of expiration date: 18 months to two years after being in a relationship with a man she developed what I call SML -- **Shagging Memory Loss**. She could rather suddenly go full hours, full DAYS, even a WEEK OR LONGER, without the thought of sex crossing her mind and when it did it floated across the theatre stage of her thoughts in a rather lovely though neutral way akin to an interest in scrapbooking or doing the crossword.

(Gentleman reader: It is important to note that I am not writing any of this from personal experience. SML is a complaint I have heard of numerous times from lesser men. This is simply me doing you a favour. My own sexual experience is quite naturally far different. Picture, if you can, a wine lover surrounded by wine barrels which he may tap whenever the mood strikes. Imagine a lover of money who sleeps on a dragon hoard of gold. Think of a pizza enthusiast who lives on a planet that is nothing but pizza moors, pizza mountains, cities of crust and sauce and sausage, pizza trees and countrysides crisscrossed by rivers of melty cheese.)

Back to SML.

And so it was that after nearly two years of being together and near constant rogering, it appeared to Adam that Eve's interest in shaggy-waggy had converted rather alarmingly and completely to a desire to engage in long, soul-crushingly detailed conversations about furniture and wall paint colour and what other people said at parties. Without any understanding of SML, Adam came to believe that to have any hope of having sex with Eve he had first pretend to be interested in home décor and mindless cocktail chatter. And with time this grim transaction betwixt man and woman became known as marriage.

If you are to be married, male reader, then you must understand from the start that the sweet, incredible and adoration-inducing interest in making the beast with two backs she will display for the first 18 to 24 months will seem to vanish utterly and harshly and unalterably. Gone, it seems. Extinct, for all appearances. Like a star fallen from the heavens which leaves a dreary, smoking hole in the earth where it will remain buried and irretrievable for all time.

Again, this deficit is how God made her, meaning, really, that this fault is no fault of her own. And one must be charitable. One must realise that a woman is essentially a man with brain damage.

They don't sprint down the gloomy, deeply unsexy path of SML with intent or any sort of self-awareness. In fact being just the tiniest bit self-centred they are extraordinarily surprised that at the moment they lose shagging memory you do not do the same. It comes as a shock that you, dear gentleman, have not changed along with them. It's as though you are two trees of the same species and when it turns autumn she loses her leaves and you do not and how strange is that?

This all might be cute except that it's demoralising.

The Shagging Memory Loss hack guaranteed to get the constant humpy-strumpy you deserve is to take the following specific step, which

you will only read of IN THIS GLORIOUS BOOK
WHICH I HAVE WRITTEN AND YOU NOW
HAVE THE GREAT FORTUNE OF READING.

Essentially you are dealing with a flaw in
her construction. Nothing more. What I am
proposing is an elegant work-around, which will
remind her of how amazing sex with you was, is,
and will ever be. (Mind you, because you are not
me, and therefore never quite the man of her
dreams, there will always be an element of
disappointment but we must lay that aside. Try not
to think of it. It will only make you sad.)

Overcoming SML will take some
preparation and a steadfastness of purpose, but next
time you are in mid-bonk and her face is flushed
and her lips are parted and swollen and she's
gasping wantonly– timing is everything – compel
her to sign a written statement declaring that yes in
fact having a lively shag with you is incredible and
that there are few things in the world that she wants
more. She will almost certainly do this if you have
left her stranded at the very moment before the
Angel Choir in her undercarriage is about to thunder
its Hallelujah chorus.

Then post that document by her side of the
bed. Having it nicely framed is always a good idea.

If possible, hire a portraitist to come in and
dash off a quick painting of the two of you enjoying
that particular jump-and-thump. Post this as a set
with the contract – even better. Some ladies are
more "visual".

The painting of the two of you in mid-
congress along with her signature at the bottom of
the contract should work some magic.

Otherwise she <u>will</u> forget. She can't help it.
This is how God made her. (Sometimes at random I

DM God and just say, "WTF Lord?!?!?" I do this on your behalf, obviously.)

And if that doesn't work and you are the despotic monarch of island nation in the 16th century, you can threaten her with imprisonment and/or grisly public execution. If however you're a peasant in any other time period, which, statistically speaking, is extremely likely, you'll simply have to drink a lot to kill the grinding sense of loss. Oh, or continue reading a book written by a certain sexy king called *Unleash Your Inner Tudor* – which will put you back on the pathway of massively gorgeous fornication, even if it's with your wife.

What We Have Learnt in Chapter 17:

- Ladies are crippled by SML and it is up to you, male person, to help her overcome this defect of the body and soul
    - Bedside contract!
    - Alcohol

Chapter 18
For the Woman Reader

Marriage – Strap in Ladies, Here Comes Glory!

Ladies, here's the truth – marriage is God's way of saying that whilst he may love you, he doesn't always like you. After six or so marriages of my own, as well as a glut of glorious mistresses and scores of super hot one-offs, I believe I have a profound and thoroughgoing understanding of the female perspective.

Six thousand years ago (more or less) when God created the world, he set out with admirable clarity of purpose, first, separating the land and the sky, oceans from the continents; he created England with all the best land and chalky-cliff bits and used all the second-rate leftover rubbish for most of Europe. When he'd truly run short of anything useful, he made Spain. On the whole, all was balance and glory.

Things took a funny little turn when it came to the business of creating man. Whilst Jehovah made all the creatures as husband/wife teams, he created man, that is Adam, on his own. Which means that like many lads, Adam enjoyed a period of being "a single man in paradise". One pictures him enjoying wrestling matches with lions, pissing contests with wolves, and getting goggle-eyed drunk with a gang of dodgy zebras. Then God interrupted all that one day by creating Eve to be his wife, who immediately began pressuring him to abandon all previous pursuits and to focus on her and her lady needs. God is thus responsible for the plotline, which goes, "youthful male happiness crushed by the tedium of marriage", which still exists even to this day. Amen.

What I'm leading up to is the following startling revelation: Your husband, has been engineered by God so that at the moment you succumb to the ravages of SML (see previous chapter), he will yearn for a time in which he was free, sex happened for him in all sort of magical and unconventional ways, and everything was shinier, better and more fantastic.

In an early draft of this book I had called this this condition **A Perfectly Reasonable Response to Marriage** (APRRM). However, after endless emails, and increasingly rude notes from my (worthless modern) editor, I have re-decided to call it **Male Mythology Syndrome** (MMS). For a "narcissistic, megalomaniacal psychopath" (not my words, obvs), I'm pretty good at compromise – WHEN I CHOOSE TO BE.

Whether or not it was true, thanks to MMS, your husband will dream of an era (pre-you) in which he was a lord of the earth, he had the strength of 10 oxen, the sexiness of a colossus, and when the bulge in his underpants was worshipped throughout the land like a holy relic whose merest touch cured disease, caused crops to grow, and the sun to emerge from behind clouds.

What can you do?

Can there possibly be a response to this?

Does anyone have an answer?

Of course, I know, and only inserted those questions for the sake of building suspense.

There are two things you can do.

First, it is important not to listen to advice from your family. Your mother or grandmother probably told you that the surest way to a man's heart is through his stomach and they said this to ensure your misery. That's how families work. The fondest wish of your parents is to make you as unhappy as they were. If not more so. That's how they win.

The surest way to a man's heart – as can be deduced through keen observation – is through his codpiece.

This is what your family did not, and will not, tell you.

You secure a man's affection by unsecuring his trousers. And then you keep, maintain and enhance his affections by:

- Dazzling at court functions
- Rendering from your stunning lady womb an abundance of male heirs
- Unleashing smoking-hot dance moves
- Pretending to disagree with your lord and husband for a bit of fun but actually wholeheartedly looking to him for all of your thoughts, ideas, emotional responses, and opinions
- Knowing how to wear hats
- Displaying courtesy to his mistress(es) – and not that icy, passive-aggressive sort of courtesy (looking at you Catherine, Anne, Jane, Anne, Kathryn and Catherine!)
- Mouth sex

The second step you can take in the face of **MMS** is that next time you are working diligently with your man on your next heir, at the moment you facilitate his fiery up-swoop into heaven, you, sweet lady, must produce and then make him sign a document that says:

- he loves & adores you
- you are the most radiant creature in all the universe

78

- he is devoted solely to you
- HIS ENTIRE BLOODY LIFE has been completely sodding improved by your very proximity

He will sign this. Why? Because these are secretly the very thoughts chasing about within his mind at the moment. It will seem as thought God himself has placed this document before him.

Finally, you will post it next to the telly box, so he will see it.

Next stop: constant joy.

What We Have Learnt in Chapter 18:
- Your family secretly wishes you to drink deep the darkness of life
- Psychopaths can compromise when it suits them
- Delusion is the source of all contentment
- Your man loves you desperately at the moment of *le petite mort*, but he is too bloody lazy to mention it

Chapter 19
When Love Goes Horribly Wrong As It Always Does Like Bloody Clockwork

Tudor Love Tip: When it comes to romance, an optimist is a pessimist in need of memory care

At my very core I am a sunny, optimistic sort with a bent toward seeing the possibilities and poetic potentialities of all persons. Because of this character flaw, Catherine of Aragon and I were man and wife for more than 20 years before it finally occurred to me that it had all turned into a lemon cake left in the road overnight during a weasel stampede.

I had hoped – in my upbeat, womb-is-half-full way – that Catherine would give England the brace of boys it required. In my darkest imaginings I could not envision a person so bereft of empathy and honour as to deny the most glorious nation in history the one thing it really couldn't live without.

Mind you, some lovely things had indeed been ticked off that list Dad had given me lo those many years ago back in Chapter 11. There had been a bit of the French invasion business. Very nice. Not Agincourt-nice but suitable. We'd been quite rude to Spain as the occasion required, though I had to tread carefully here – the wife's family and what-what. We had burnt bits of Scotland. Fantastic. The Pope had given me a "Defender of the Faith" award, which sat on my desk looking shiny and terrific.

But some keenly important dynasty propagation bits were still left undone. Not for lack of trying, mind you. At least on my part.

What it came down to is that Catherine's womb was Spanish. It looked Spanish. It only truly responded to commands delivered in Spanish. And I swear if you put your ear to it you could hear street music of Barcelona. Given its political and cultural leanings, her vagina refused steadfastly to give England the one and really the only thing England absolutely required.

Male heirs.

Oh, it managed to cough up a girl, of course. Mary. (OMG!!)

Meaning that not only was her womb a traitor, it was being derisive as well.

Dark clouds. Very dark clouds.

Catherine became fanatically defensive of her unyielding paella pan. There were words. Rash and rude. She began spending more time in her chapel with God and I began spending more time in the bedchamber with my mistress, Bessie Blount.

By noticeable contrast to Catherine, Bessie's uterus displayed moving patriotism by producing a lovely, healthy bastard son whom I named Henry Fitzroy.

As I held the damp, squishy boy child, I realised little Fitzroy was more than a son. He was a message. Probably from my departed parents up in heaven waving their shimmering, semi-transparent arms, trying to tell me that the problem was obviously not with my Tudor heir-making prowess but that of my wife's.

I'd spent 20 years planting English seed in a disinterested and increasingly gloomy Spanish orchard. The sort of thing from which we derive the terms "fruitless venture". Might as well try to burn coal to make steam to operate an engine that could transport people and goods by rail. Ridiculous.

It was at this time the little, rasping voice in the back of my mind reminded me that the Holy

Bible exhorts one not to lay with your brother's wife – that the result of doing so would be a childless union.

I suppose from the modern perspective it was not a childless marriage, because of Mary, but from the perspective of a 16th-century English monarch – which is the correct perspective – it was pretty freaking childless.

Having an only-daughter as my heir would be the equivalent of needing a warhorse on the day of battle and being presented with a unicycle.

And where, I tried to remember, had I received this idea that the Godly exhortation about wedding a brother's wife didn't apply to me???

My sweet and lovely mum?

The privy council?

Any of the hoards of unwashed peasants who cheered and praised me constantly?

Jesus up in heaven?

My own fantastic brain?

Oh that's right, it was the Pope. The Pope in bleeding Rome.

It was pretty clear to me now that the Pope had given me some bad information.

Wow. What now?

Here are the five stages of grief when your 40-year-old immigrant wife refuses to give you the right sort of baby:

1. denial
2. anger
3. alcohol/binge eating
4. new mistress
5. annulment

Have you noticed what one of the stages was not? If you said "eating a pony" you are probably six-year-old Edward VI. The answer I am looking for is "fall in love". If that was your response, you are correct and should award yourself something nice.

That's right. Falling in love when your heart has just been bicycle-kicked into Life's gawping football net of sadness is not the thing.

At all.

Write this down on a card and keep it with you always.

I did not and it bit me in the codpiece.

What we have learnt in Chapter 19
- Beware the sarcastic uterus
- Even after they're dead, parents still have things they wish to say and will say them in awkward and oddly inappropriate ways
- Someone seriously needs to create a dating app that rates ladies on their womb's likelihood of disgorging boys

Expand Your Vocabulary, Enlarge Your World

Vagican:
When the Vatican gets all up in one's lady business

Chapter 20
It is better to have loved and lost than to have dated Anne Boleyn

Tudor Relationship Tip: If she's not doing rumpity pumpity in your bed, believe me, she's doing rumpity pumpity to your head

One evening in the Great Hall at Hampton Court fires were ablaze, a thousand candles lit and wine flowed like most liquids do when poured and in pranced the second daughter of Thomas and Elizabeth Boleyn fresh from the French court – and believe me most ladies do not return from the French court looking anything less than ridden very hard and put away with their damp saddles still upon them.

Anne B was a slim, fit, raven-haired young thing with eyes that promised everything. And when I say everything I specifically mean sex. The sort of sex that includes snacks afterward and then more sex.

We danced. She flirted relentlessly. I had to have her.

Her sister, Mary, a sweet, kind, and widely beloved slut had been my mistress (as her mother had been lo those many years prior) giving up her fleshly gifts cheerfully and substantially.

Naturally I expected Anne would have the same leisurely, languorous, wantonness as Mary's though perhaps without Mary's run-of-the-mill ignorance and addiction to puns.

Late into the night as we danced. Our eyes locked and hers seemed to say that I should unharness that big royal codpiece of mine and see what dreamy, dreamy wonders would come to pass.

Hardly able to breathe, I drew Anne into an antechamber and began to disassemble my codpiece as her eyes had so clearly instructed, when she stopped me.

She insisted, with her mouth nearly on mine, that I could have her only when she was my wife. Wait, *what*? I drew back and looked into at her eyes, which were indeed clearly still demanding an immediate appointment with my man bits.

In total bewilderment I looked from her eyes and back to her mouth, which just at that moment whispered, "Wife."

Eyes and mouth only inches apart and yet in such total dispute.

I preferred the eyes, obvs. Yet they remained the mute, pleading, second-in-command to the lips.

Well, and, I was pretty sure the mouth was in complete command of the reality that I had a wife – who was even at that moment in her private chapel fingering her rosary beads, ignoring her baby making duties, growing rotund, and starting to smell like old people.

"Erm," I stammered. "Well perhaps I could finish taking off my codpiece and just see what happens."

Her thin white hand grasped my shoulder.

"I hear you like to hunt," she said in that alto voice that made my heart get hot and oozy like a tuna melt.

"I do like the hunt," I said, being exceedingly clever. See what I did there?

"Then tomorrow, we hunt."

Her eyes now seemed to again promise everything, only tomorrow, whilst hunting. So changeable, yet so fiery, so alluring, so other-adjectives-that-also-meant-alluring.

I could have invented internal combustion right there.

Thus it began. A long period, a very, very long period of my life in which I did not, for I could not, shag the one person I truly, madly, deeply wished to. And the longer I did not lead an invasionary force into her knickers the more desperate I became. So desperate I actually kept a daily journal devoted solely to this "great matter".

Here are excerpts:

- Journal of Not Shagging Anne Boleyn, Day 1

"Feeling good. Anne & I went hunting. By Christ how she rides a horse. Clenching her strong thighs about its thickness. A gleam of sweat on her mouth, her brow reddening and tightening with the exertion. The wind catching her French hood, flinging it off. Crikey. She says we must wait until we are wed. Of course she's right. I shall have sex later with her sister Mary and think on Anne's beauty & virtue."

- Journal of Not Shagging Anne Boleyn, Day 2

"Went with A. for a perambulation about the pond. My hand brushed the front of her dress. Felt the heat and the outer contour of her warm, womanly mound. Or thought I did. No, I did. I'm king, I know things. The 'No Shagging Rule' still in place. As it should be. Ouch, my undercrackers."

- Journal of Not Shagging Anne Boleyn, Day 3

Bloody hell.

- Journal of Not Shagging Anne Boleyn, Week 2

Feast. Pageant. God's wounds, I swear her lady parts have a voice, the sweet, musical call of a dove. "I'm here your Majesty. Right here. Separated from you by a stretch of cloth, the thickness of a feather."

- Journal of Not Shagging Anne Boleyn, Week 3

Going into dinner A. let me touch her neck. Frisson. Stepped outside for a mo and rogered a pile of leaves. Emergency.

- Journal of Not Shagging Anne Boleyn, Month 3

Sent Bessie Blount an emerald ring with the word Jericho inscribed within the band. She knew what to do. Met me at my so-named hunting lodge where ladies' knickers, like the Biblical town walls, come tumbling down.

- Journal of Not Shagging Anne Boleyn, Month 6

Massive ball ache. Had to return to my wife's bedchamber. Closed eyes and thought of England. A. not happy but Aragon IS MY SODDING WIFE! She still sits beside me at state functions. She still prays for my soul & mends my shirts. She still performs her bedchamber duties even if she does so with the frozen look of someone watching a church burn.

- Journal of Not Shagging Anne Boleyn, Year 2, Month 8, Day 27

Can't take this. She lets me undress her. Kiss her. Touch her. But the best part of me cannot come in contact with the best part of her. Torture. Agony. Dark angels every where. Who must I behead to clear my mind? Who must I burn? Hang? Disembowel? All is warped by misery. I suppose years from now they'll say I had personality disorder or that I was psychotic. Hopefully someone will have the kindness to realise that not shagging Anne Boleyn MADE ME MENTAL! It's her fault! AAAAAAHHHHH Sweet Jesus up a Banana Tree, I CANNOT GO ON!

- Journal of Not Shagging Anne Boleyn, Year 4, Month 6, Day 15

Numb. Completely numb. Can't think. Can't feel sensation of any sort. Today at the joust I left the visor on my helmet up so the Duke of Suffolk's lance could smash me in the face. Just to let me feel something.

Six agonising years this horrible, brittle, crippling, virtuous behaviour went on and on, driving me into deeper and more appalling circles of hell. It was poisoning me, toxic to those around me, yea, the kingdom itself seemed struck with a gargantuan case of inflamed scrotum.

And whilst keeping my ship out of her lady harbour for six years, Anne always coyly and confidently insinuated that the hardship of the journey would be more than rewarded by the destination.

Six years of kisses and arse grabs and codpiece wiggles all coming with the promise of more riches than could be imagined on its way. Much more. Whatever I could picture in my royal mind, sex with Anne Boleyn was going to exceed THAT.

Once I lay with my head in her lap and asked, "Will it be better than eating cheese?"

"Yes," she replied. "Much better."

"Will it be better than eating cheese whilst drinking wine?"

"Oh indeed my love," Anne whispered, "It will be better than that."

"Will it be more fantastic than hurling Spaniards from the Tower whilst eating cheese and drinking wine and shagging your sister?"

She made a funny gurgly noise in her throat just then but managed, "Verily, far finer."

And so it went. One promise heaped upon another each more golden than the last.

Now, let us pause a moment to reflect on this. Ladies – if you keep a king waiting half a dozen years to take an amble through your Hanging Gardens of Babylon, you had better be concealing all the glories of a Roman orgy, the beauty of 1,000 sunsets, and the wonders of freaking Narnia down there. If you do, that's how fairytales are made. But if you do not – and this is the more likely of the two outcomes – you might as well just shoot an email to the Swordsman of Calais yourself.

What We Have Learnt in Chapter 20
- Six years in the friend zone is like being a human GIF of an exploding scrotum, blowing up every 4 seconds

- Over-promising in the vagina department does not
typically end well
- Gurgly noise

Your Tudor Weekly Plan

Thursday:
- Roar
- Swagger
- Thrust your chin
- Strike impressive poses
- Suddenly sweep things off desk
- Shout "THIS MEANS WAR!"
- Cake
- More shouting
- More cake
- Crossword

Chapter 21
My Sexity Brexity

*Tudor Leadership Tip: Make your Brexit about a
quest for love. And money and power, obvs. But
keep the focus on love, it'll make it easier to sell to
television.*

In 2016 UK voters broke with the powers of
the European Union in Brussels, escaping a vast,
ugly scheme in which dodgy foreigners took British
money and told the good people of England how to
live their lives.

While this Brexit was obviously the right
thing to do, it was of course entirely unoriginal.

Because I did it first.

Nearly 500 years prior, our version of the
European Union was the Catholic Church of Rome.
The Pope took money from all the nations of
Europe – literally collected taxes, occupied
buildings (churches, monasteries, etc.) on their land,
and told everyone what to do. And I don't just mean
peasants and merchants, as you might expect, I
mean actual people, such as rich people and
monarchs.

If a king – a sexy, ginger sociopath, we'll
say – wanted a divorce from a wholly unsuitable
Spanish wife, he had to beg the Pope in Rome for
permission. Beg. Demand. Negotiate. Bribe.
Scheme. Hold councils. Work behind the schemes
to drum up support.

And after all that the Pope might – or might
not – say 'yes' depending on the whim of the
moment.

Madness.

Even so, this is the way the world had worked for literally 1,000 years. The Church of Rome had essentially picked up where ancient Rome had left off. One empire exchanged for another. It had its abbeys, monasteries, priories, nunneries, schools, and chapels and churches spread throughout the whole of Europe like a web of organised crime. And in my 16th century the church was in expansion mode, setting up shop in unsuspecting bits of the Americas, Africa, and Asia.

The church had its hoary, aeons-old talons sunk deep into the hearts, souls, and coin purses of everyone in Christendom.

Now, it takes a shrewd and original mind to eyeball a thing that is assumed by absolutely everyone to be proper and traditional and say to oneself, "What if this thing were not a thing?" Then to add, "And how could unmaking this thing get me the lady benefits I need whilst at the same time make me gobsmackingly rich?"

When it first became clear that to have Anne I should have to break off my 20-year marriage with Catherine, I began by instructing my chancellor, Cardinal Wolsey, to make discreet inquiries in Rome about arranging a tidy little divorce with the Pope – based on the idea that I had slept with my brother's wife and according to the Bible had no business marrying her in the first place. (I also stepped up my relationship game by checking in with the Pope on one other Old Testament-related item about marriage but you'll have to wait until Chapter 24 to fully comprehend just how amazingly I had finally begun to unleash my own inner Tudor! It's brilliant – very exciting!! Can't wait to tell you!!). Anyway, this was in 1527. I wasn't quite prepared to deal with Catherine flapping about the palace screaming like a seagull so hoped to keep all this on the down-low.

Eventually – and I mean after years of tiresome and tedious back and forth – Wolsey couldn't do the deal with the Pope and in a frenzied rage I drove him from court and he died because he could not stop shitting himself. True story.

Catherine of course refused to cooperate. There's much she could have done to make this whole thing easier on me (which is to say, easier on England!!). Could have whisked herself off to a nunnery to be as religious and non-sexual as she pleased. Could have interceded with the Pope to grant my annulment. She might have died. But no. Instead she declared herself my one true wife and England's one true queen, grew very wide in the bottom, and refused to budge. The most passive-aggressive act in all of history.

By 1531 I couldn't take the sight of her any longer, and with the help of my new chief minister Thomas Cromwell and numerous henchmen and to the ear-splitting sounds of her protestations, Catherine was pried off her throne and banished from court. I had her carted away to a drafty, disease-y, old castle somewhere north, where, fingers crossed, I truly hoped she'd slurp into a swamp never to be see again.

I then petitioned the Pope myself and when that didn't work, I simply did my own Brexit. Told the Pope and his entire network of lies and Popish poopery to piss off.

In February 1531 with the rubber stamp of the English clergy and later by Parliament – thanks, chaps – I named myself head of what I wanted to call The Glorious Church of the Super Amazing and Wonderfully Virile Henry VIII, but was talked out of it. For the best, I suppose. Eventually it became the succinctly named Church of England. I sent around a very impressive piece of vellum that all monks, priests, abbots, and holy persons needed to sign that agreed with me on my being in charge of this new religion. And being the person who got to wear all the related sparkly bits and the special hat and so forth. Those who did not sign were presented with a menu of options, the most pleasant of which was starving to death in prison. The other choices got exceedingly nasty from there. I was forced to behead non-signers including Thomas More and Bishop Fisher to finally win their support.

Well, it's human nature. People hate change. Even good change. So the *Unleash Your Inner Tudor* leadership hack embedded here is if you want to get loads of people readily joining you on any journey – and not fighting you at every turn – it's best to have a handful of them hanged, drawn, and quartered. #InspiredLeadership

To complete this church business, I needed a "Primate of All England," a title which makes plain my intention to install a monkey as Archbishop. When I couldn't find a suitable creature, I gave the job to the Boleyn family chaplain Thomas Cranmer, who worked out nicely.

I then began to plunder all of the Pope's property in England enriching myself and the crown with lands, gold, silver, gems and other nice bits. And then I began to purge the land of Papists by having them burnt.

At last, all was in readiness to have sex with Anne.

What We Have Learnt in Chapter 21
- Only the best and brightest turn a break-up into a moneymaking venture
- Don't call it plunder, call it reformation
- It might be a red flag if you have to work this hard to get a lady to have sex with you #JustSaying

Chapter 22
On Finally Making Rumpity Pumpity With Anne Boleyn Following a Wait of Six Years

Tudor Love Tip: Good things do come to those who wait. But unbelievably horrible things come to those who wait, too. So, waiting is not a guarantee of quality.

Now that I was supreme head of my own church and could clear my name and hers of sin, Anne and I were free at last to pound our pancetta.

And so it was whilst on holiday/a business trip in France, in the town of Calais in 27 October 1532, we got drunk and did it.

Of course it was in every way different from any noodle-doodle you have known. I am king, after all.

Oh, bloody hell, who am I fooling? How was sex with Anne Boleyn, you ask? With all those spidery elbows and slashing shoulder blades and those collar bones smashing me in the face like bronze knuckles? I swear by Christ she had more bones than the average person and all of them sharpened at the tips. It was like trying to impregnate a box of pencils.

She, on the other hand, clearly thought she was in the midst of carrying out a thing of universe-shattering magnificence – throwing her arms about and squishing her eyes shut so the skin went micro-wrinkled and white and barring her overlong teeth. Painful. Like watching Richard III think.

At one point I am certain Anne was on the point of bursting into song and she looked at me in a side-eye, checking-the-temperature-of-the-room sort of way and I just said, "Don't". I would have involuntarily thrown her through the window. Anyway, it ended. Thank merciful God.

What do you do when you've finally gone all the way and it's simply a two or three on the one-to-ten scale? Maybe a four. If you're me at this point in my life you hang on to a tiny spark of hope, a shiny bit of youthful optimism deep down in your soul, shining like a candle in the wind, thinking, "Perhaps this will get better ... surely this is not the Promised Land sweet Anne has promised lo these many years whilst I was tortured by thirst and hunger in the sexual wilderness".

But after six years, I may have built up too much resentment, bewilderment, and outrage to find Anne's booty pleasures enjoyable. After all, what sort of person could have sex and doesn't? Who allows even a single day of life pass without choosing joy?

As I see it, we each of us have two trees that grow within the gardens of our lives. One is the Tree of Joy heavy with its succulent, honeyed fruits of pleasure dangling from its aromatic branches. The fruit includes binge eating, seducing ladies, buying new clothes, invading France, wine, jumping up and down on one's bed, roast beef, cheese, reckless pie eating, plundering monasteries, writing amazing poetry, more pies, and yes obviously sex, etc.

Then there is the Tree of the Mundane, which has no fruit at all, only a scattering of dry, shriveled leaves. These limp, tasteless leaves include toil, not eating cake on a daily basis, getting out of bed too early, not having a mistress, dreary hours not shouting at people who ought to be shouted at, having your children around all the time, accounting, and not having sex.

Anne had for the past six years chosen the Tree of the Mundane over the Tree of Joy even while the Tree of Joy stood well within her reach.

Who does that?

It's clearly someone who does not understand the shortness of life on this Earth (and in the 16th century this was very brief indeed). Or it's someone for whom having a good time is not their idea of having a good time.

In addition, there is a difference between not having sex and withholding sex. Not having sex is typically the result of lack of opportunity. Or a health issue such as a bad back or a dodgy sausage. Withholding sex, such as Anne had done, means that one is perfectly capable of it but for a variety of ugly and indecipherable reasons elects not to.

Six years of being denied a thing easily given builds up quite a sizeable wave of dark thoughts within one.

Beyond all that, I was now half a dozen years older and my loin-related tastes had changed. I found myself attracted to women with a good deal more pudding on their bones.

And yet, there was still this poisonous optimism inside me.

"Give it a go," I thought.

And so I did what you do when you're filled with sunniness and good thoughts, you go at it a few more times, in a few more places, until you realise that no, there is no reason to hope. None. It's going to be bad and that's all. You've waited six years expecting the moon and instead you've received a deformed octopus wrapped in a dirty napkin. And in spite of all evidence that this will

100

not go well, you do still have a stubborn bit of sanguinity left within and you marry her anyway. You did start a church for her after all. You suffer through the daily trials of a soul-wasting relationship, your ex-wife dies and the doctors do an autopsy and find that her heart is black as tar (like I didn't already know that) – not making this up – you gaze across the supper table at your one legit heir, a girl named Mary who seems not to like you one tiny bit, and yet still you're too kind and sensitive and filled with poetry and predictability to know quite what to do. And then God steps in once again to give you just what you need – as a husband, father, boyfriend, and tyrant. And he does it at a joust.

What We Have Learnt in Chapter 22
- Six years is too long by about 28 centuries
- Acting like you're amazing in bed and being amazing in bed are not the same
- As my dad once said "Patience is a virtue that will always hurt you"
- Choose joy

Expand Your Relationship Vocabulary, Enlarge Your World

Sistress:
When your wife's sister is your mistress

Chapter 23
Leadership is inside you waiting to be
unleashed through the magic of violent injury

*Tudor Leadership Tip: There is the sort of
leadership that relies on terrifying everyone and
there's the other kind. Can't think what that one is.*

God has a plan for each of us.

His plan for you is, I'm going to guess, that
you breed, pay your taxes in full, and work toward
the interests of the ruling class in your principality
or region.

In the case of monarchs, such as my glorious
self, God sets a rather high bar. Like you, we are
indeed intended to procreate. But unlike you we are
also meant to look impressive and august on a
balcony, tell people what to do, invade, plunder,
smash bits of foreign countries, and look pretty
incredible in gold underpants. In my case, however,
God had set that already high monarchical bar miles
higher. I simply couldn't comprehend in my first 30
years of life quite how high it was, that it was in
fact a higher height than any previous king had been
asked to even dream of reaching. Eventually I
would learn that the Almighty, in his wisdom and
majesty, wished for me to become the obese, gouty,
megalomaniacal, merciless tyrant that England,
verily, that history itself, and various historians who
host television shows, needed. And I clearly wasn't
getting there unaided.

The Lord's gentle guidance first came to me
in 1524 when at a jousting tournament I failed to
lower the visor on my helmet and charged full
speed at my opponent's lance taking the wooden tip
straight to the face.

I recall lying amid sawdust and horse turds wondering what message our sweet Saviour and/or his dad was trying to send.

That didn't do the trick so a year later, I was knocked senseless when I landed head first in a brook whilst trying to vault across it with a pole. As one does.

On that occasion I was rather upside down with a great wound shouting "Speak to me oh Lord for I am listening!" I was indeed trying to hear our Lord's sweet whisperings but these kinds of events tend to stir up quite a lot of noise – footmen shouting for help, horses hooves from in-coming nobles, various babblings, cries of "The King Liveth!" and blah, blah, blah.

Still not quite picking up what Jehovah was laying down, a third incident occurred at a jousting tournament at Greenwich Palace on 24 January 1536 when I was on the receiving end of an incoming lance and was hurled from my horse in full armour. The horse, also in full armour, landed on top of me. I lay as one dead and everyone freaked out, believing I had gone off prematurely to be with Jesus.

This was God working his miraculous ways.

In my other-worldly, head-wounded semi-consciousness I could at last hear the voice of God and I felt cuddled and cradled by the singing of his dreamy, sweet song, "Lights will guide you home … And ignite your bones … and I will try to fix you …" (The words were later co-opted by Coldplay to lesser effect.)

When I blurred back to this world – to the astonishment of all who had already begun to fight about who would be the next king – I awoke to a completely different perspective on everything, thanks to Jehovah updating my brain's operating system.

For the whole of my kingship I had been known for being intelligent, fun-loving, and even-tempered. I had been the cheerfully benign boss, the cool dad, the teacher who is more friend than adult and who buys you cannabis, takes you camping, and then does not try to have sex with you. And what had that gotten me?

NOT!

BLOODY!

MUCH!!

I'd been misled by one Pope about the validity of my first marriage and greatly arsed about by another regarding my urgently needed annulment. I'd been annoyed, deceived, and endlessly harried by France and Spain. I'd gotten nothing but mischief and knavery from Scotland.

I'd enjoyed historic and histrionic levels of disenchantment from one of the finest uteruses in all Europe (or thus it had been advertised by Spain) and now the English lady I'd taken up with was pulling me by the hand down a narrow, thorny path to a damp, melancholy little village, where our future together dwelt, called Sadness-Upon-Shittington.

As I drifted back into consciousness I was not filled with the wonderment of being alive, but instead was bursting with the idea that to achieve my dreams from this moment forward I would need to sprout wings and power myself into the heavenly heavens by carbo-loading a new fuel called rage.

To conquer the dragon, one must become the fucking dragon.

As I recuperated in my bedchamber I began to try out the new tools for leadership that God had placed before me like so many prezzies on Christmas morning. These included explosive anger, implacable ill-temper, and irrational demands whilst dancing about from being impulsive to aggressive to impulsive again to neurotic to full-throttle bonkers. I even began to try them on in combination.

I would begin the day, for example, by shouting instructions to the Privy Council about one direction to head with Spain, watch them fly about executing my orders and then after lunch I would feign a complete change of heart and totally re-write my foreign policy. I would slather thick, delicious icing on the day by launching into an incandescent tirade about the foolhardy work they had done in the morning as though I'd utterly forgotten the orders I had given at breakfast. Haha.

Did I become a giant turd? A twat? A tyrant. Oh sweet Lord I did, I did, I did. And at the same time, I became effective. I got things done. Because one did not simply follow my orders, one praised them, licked their boots, nibbled lovingly at their necks and made sweet love to them – and repeated this performance when I called for orders that were utterly contradictory.

Leadership, in short, is about being volatile and scary and frankly, the more you have the ability to have people legally killed, the more they'll listen to you, do whatever you say, meet deadlines, and say nice things to you.

What We Have Learnt in Chapter 23
- Those who you, sweet reader, see as evil despots
see themselves as national heroes beset on all sides
by traitors, time-wasters, numbskulls, and idiots
- If you're not shouting, they're not hearing you
- Being greedy, sex-addicted, sociopathic, and
megalomaniacal are nothing more than basic
leadership skills
- Brain trauma your way to success

Tudor Trust Exercise

Team-building is important in any era. A great
exercise is to choose a partner and fall backward
into their arms, crushing them under your weight.

Chapter 24
The Queen is Dead, Long Live the Queen

Tudor Love Tip: Treat your love life as a business.
Have goals, strategies, and dangle the promise of
sex with the boss as a means of advancement.

It was a new era; I was at long last on the
path to perfection and there were problems to get
sorted. Number one on my list: "How Do You
Solve a Problem Like Anne Boleyn?" Which didn't
quite work as a song. Nor as a marriage.

Anne had managed, like her predecessor
Catherine, to propel just one baby from her lady
blowpipe and it was a girl – did I say it was a girl?
It was a girl. Who we named Elizabeth and for
whom I saw little future beyond marrying off to
secure a fishing treaty with Norway.

So here I was in 1536 at the age of 45 and
had not crossed a rather important item – in fact
THE important item – off the list of king things I
must do. You lot in your shiny wifi era think
nothing of a successful man starting a family in his
mid-40s. Well, dear modern persons, I faced very
different facts.

My dad, Henry VII, who was careful about
diet and exercise was dead at the age of 52. Overall
the average lifespan of the King Henrys of England
was 52.7 years, making dad distressingly ordinary.
The average age of a King Edward was 45.4 years
whilst that of a Richard was a paltry 34 (some of
that skewed by my dad's handiwork at Bosworth!!)

If we go by the Henry averages, I had at best
seven years to sire man babies in order to keep
England glorious via more Tudor throne magic.

I was under pressure – heir pressure, one might say – as never before. And Anne Boleyn's hapless va-jay-jay wasn't helping.

What now?

If you picture me as quite flummoxed and rather at a loss and sitting by a Hampton Court window staring out at grey Surrey clouds with tears in my eyes, then perhaps you should begin this book again because a Tudor always learns from his missteps.

Let's begin with ye olde traditional Tudor saying, "Give me a girl heir once, shame on you, give me a girl heir twice, shame on me."

I had learnt brilliantly from the debacle of my first marriage and back in Chapter 21 had applied that learning to the second – but had done so in secret! (Though I sometimes shouted about it very loudly in my head.)

Now I found myself searching madly for that very secret to my possible escape amongst my books and papers, where I was sure I'd hidden it.

I tore through my personal effects until I found a small envelope closed with a wax seal with my face and some nice words in Latin. On the outside of the envelope I had written in quill, "In Case Things Go Badly with Anne B".

I ripped it open and inside was written a short verse from the Bible:

– which I had jotted down and tucked away a full eight years prior

– because I am a brilliant strategist

– as we shall see!

Over the course of the next few days and weeks, I discussed this verse with any number of learned men, religious types just curious, obviously, if there were any possibility my marriage with Anne was as cursed as had been my marriage to Catherine of Aragon.

Turns out there was – according to the non-paid, non-compelled consensus. And my escape route opened before me.

To fully explore this brilliant marriage hack, we must journey back in time to 1528.

I had written to Pope Clement VII just to make sure it'd be ok Bible-wise and Jesus-wise to marry a woman (Anne) who was the sister of one of my mistresses (Mary)? I mean, should I ever want to. Not saying I'm going to. I was married already, *naturellement*. Just on the off chance, etc.

Clement, who would go on to refuse to give me an annulment to Catherine of Aragon, nonetheless came back with the answer that everything would be fine with God on this one. No problemo.

Though this was exactly the answer I was hoping to hear, I had been fooled by a Pope once before in this regard and I decided that rather than be blindsided by God's tricky commands down the road, I would tuck this little Bible verse away just in case I should ever need it as an excuse for divorce.

The verse all this hangs on is located in that great stewpot of a book in the Bible, Leviticus, chapter18, verse 18. It quotes Jehovah as instructing: "Thou shall not marry a woman in addition to her sister as a rival while she is alive, to uncover her nakedness."

I know. To the modern reader this sounds like the sort of haiku one writes after consuming a spicy eels and an opium ball.

It meant simply that the Lord "His Awesomeness" Jehovah said that since I'd repeatedly and fantastically slept with Mary Boleyn

– "uncovering her nakedness" – making her sister, Anne, my wife was indeed **not** an option and that my marriage to her was illegitimate as well as an outright abomination.

Sorry, Jesus.

When all of this came together I jumped up and down on my bed until I was out of breath and perspiring with my heart pounding in my throat.

Thomas Cromwell, my chief minister as I have mentioned, watched this outburst of joy with his usual detachment.

"Oh TCrom, I shall need to pretend to be sad about this when I deliver the news to her," I said. "I shall need to quiver my chin and make my eyes damp. It will be wonderful!"

"Your majesty, I wonder if …" he said and then didn't.

"What it is?"

"Nothing your majesty."

"Look, you can't begin a sentence with words and then end it with ellipses and expect me to let it go," I said.

"Well," he said, "I just wonder if it's enough. That's all."

"If what is enough?"

"Hanging the entirety of your divorce – well, your possible divorce – on a single Bible verse. Again."

"Again? What are you saying?"

"You know how people are."

"Spit it out man!"

"Second marriage, second daughter, second time a divorce is demanded based on a verse in Leviticus."

"BLOODY HELL YOU'RE NOT SAYING I'M BORING!!!"

I had now descended from the bed filled with rage, feeling like a minotaur must feel all the time.

TCrom shrank back appropriately.

"Well, your majesty, you can see how it could be interpreted by some – not by me of course – but by some, peasants mostly and lady historians, as a done-that-been-there move."

"A Tudor is never boring," I said, calming a bit.

"Everyone knows that."

"And this Bible verse thing, it's solid."

"Completely solid."

"But obviously I would never repeat myself."

"Obviously."

"That was never my plan."

"Tremendous," he said.

"My plan was ... erm ... my plan ..."

"A show trial and a beheading?" Cromwell suggested.

"Well ..."

"Perhaps she's had sex with quite a number of men in the court."

"Really?"

"Including her brother."

"How very tasteless."

"And a musician."

"WHAT!?"

"And she has spoken ill of your poetry. She has laughed at it."

The room began to spin, my vision went scarlet. I think for a moment I literally exploded.

"Do what needs to be done," I croaked from my foetal position on the floor. "Right this wrong, dear fellow."

One does not mock my poetry.

And so Cromwell texted the Swordsman of Calais and set about with cheerful clarity of purpose to set up Anne's trial and eventual end. Whilst he was busy with the business of beheading, I was consumed with the details of my wedding. Oh, did I not mention that I was once again in love? But indeed. The new brain the Lord had given me was quite capable of managing the end of one relationship and the magical start of another.

A Tudor multitasks, as discussed.

I have always been a great ship sailing upon the Sea of Love and always will be.

Romance is a wonderful thing.

What we have learnt in Chapter 24

- Throughout history more great solutions have been dreamt of whilst jumping up and down on a bed than most historians are willing to admit

- Don't ask God to take away your problems, ask him to take away your hesitancy to use violence to solve them

- Beware the hapless va-jay-jay

**Expand Your Relationship Vocabulary, Enlarge
Your World**

Monogamish:
*When you are completely and entirely faithful to a
spouse more or less.*

Your Tudor Weekly Plan

Friday:

- Practise cruel tyrant look
- Practise storming about
- Work on booming laugh
- Practise the opposite of chastity
- A lot
- Cheese orgy

Chapter 25

In Which I Show Actual Concern About The Sorts of Choices You're Making

Tudor Love Tip: Marriage is so often a perfectly good love affair spoiled

One thing you lot have given up on – to your detriment – is the arranged marriage. It is alarming how this concept has become the target of booing and mockery in your era. You're on a slippery slope, modern persons. What's next -- rescinding the Buggery Act of 1536?

The arranged marriage is an institution that faces actual bleeding facts: a man needs at least two women in his life:

A) the careworn, penny-pinching, child-rearing drab who stage-manages the household and;

B) the pretty, carefree bit of smoochy-pants who loves to touch his cheek and pinch his bum, circulate her lithe alluring bits about his purview, have a laugh, and who treats sex with him as sunlight for the soul.

A man needs both.

And you do not get both of the above ladies in the same person. (My editor has insisted that I insert a paragraph here on the wondrous complexity of ladies because apparently celebrating the wondrous complexity of ladies is likely to sell more books. To ladies. And I'm supposed to say something positive about Oprah.)

If a man is monogamous and stays with just one woman he gets the second one first for a short while and then is stuck with the first one for a distressingly long time.

Your forbearers, who you like to picture as monstrous barbarians, knew of all this and created the arranged marriage. Acquiring a wife through arranged marriage was no more indebted to emotional attachment than it would be to sign a celebrated striker for a football team. It's a deal, a business contract, a marketing strategy, the bringing together of two houses to a mutually advantageous end. Once the dowry is agreed upon, the wife impregnated, the thing is off and running like things that operate well when they have oil in them [need better metaphor here]. Then the man, having provided for the logistics of his household and career and dynasty, is free to enjoy a discreet bit on the side to keep his jingle bells a jingle-jing-jingling.

The arranged marriage is the response to the very real reality that men have binary needs throughout their lives, a dual allegiance to head and to throbbly-wobbly bits. The head is about the raising of children and the creating of a household as a profit-centre, which will pass on great benefit to his heirs. The rest is about wiener magic.

As far as I can tell, women don't have this as they are only one person at a time. From approximately 18 to 28 years of age they are the lovely bit of fun who likes to have a drink and a dance and all manner of intemperate exuberance until dawn. And then from 28 onward they perform one of nature's most depressing transformations, turning from butterfly to caterpillar, yearning, burning, it seems to become the beleaguered drudge with an increasingly debilitating case of Shagging Memory Loss.

Who would choose to be the dark cloud when one could be the sunlight? It argues for the idea that it's not a thing ladies get to decide. It's simply how God made them, which is a disappointment. Though perhaps it's a mercy in disguise, intended to make the inevitability of death seem more attractive.

Not that I have anything against the drudge. Every man needs a Cromwell who will keep things brisk and tidy and have things stolen for you or people who may or may not be technically guilty of anything hurled into dungeons as the occasion warrants.

Even though I know there's no changing your minds on this one I must in the name of kindness at least mention the advantages of the arranged marriage, as my life is a towering, living testament.

Do as you will. Make your mistakes. Don't blame this book for your suffering.

What We Have Learnt in Chapter 25
- Men have needs that are as grandly unchanging as glorious craggy cliffs, which stand as regal sentinels over the dark sea of life
- Women evolve over time like coins, going from bright and shiny to dull and bitter if you touch your tongue to them
- The wondrous complexity of ladies/Oprah

Expand Your Relationship Vocabulary, Enlarge Your World

Relationslip:
Oops, I did it again

Chapter 26
Letters from Readers

Dear King Henry VIII,
    I have a lady what I want to make a baby with and she's putting me off. And she's a Papist. What should I do?
    Warmest regards,
    Average Bloke

Dear Bloke,
    As a Papist you'll need to have her sent round to Smithfield so we can have her burnt.
    Majestically,
    HR

My Most Majestic Liege, Lord & King,
    There is a wealthy, powerful gentleman, a member of the nobility, whom I would wish to give the glories of my body and thus produce for him a male heir –

Dear Lady Whose Letter I Cannot Finish Reading,
    There are limits to what the male human can withstand. Your letter is simply far too sexy. If I were to read even one word further, I would likely do a grievous injury to my person.
    In some discomfort,
    HR

    My Most Majestic Sovereign King and Grace,
    The man whom I love for his lands, money and power has slept with my sister and I <u>think</u> with my mum. My plan is to marry him and mock his

dancing, poetry and ability to please me in bed and to have sex with loads of chavs and probably have a baby but not a boy. Oh, and I'll be a witch.

Feeling pretty confident this will all work out just fine. What do you think?

Anne Boleyn

Dear Anne,
Don't be a dick.
Most sincerely,
HR

Chapter 27
The Thing About Happiness Is That It Should be Called "Pre-Kicking You in The Balls"

*Tudor Love Tip: Before the grim end, stage-manage
a bright new beginning*

By 1536 my heart had been crushed not once but twice like a banana in a large machine specifically designed to pulp non-European fruits. Although in the case of Cath of A it was the extended dance version of crushing, over the course of two decades or more, so it was less about shock and pain and more about "Sweet Christ in a donkey costume this is annoying and slow."

With Anne Boleyn, the wounding of my heart took less time but it was hardly a blur.

Most often having your heart made into a mince meat pie does not come as a total surprise. If you're truly honest with yourself, you can admit having seen the large grinding machine coming for you at some distance. The *Unleash Your Inner Tudor* romance hack I've always found best – take note, sweet reader – is to always be lining up your next life-changing love affair before the current one has gone tits up.

What you want is ***overlap***.

Like one of those Venn Diagrams where the light blue circle is Lady Now and the light green circle is Lady Next and in that place where they lay one atop the other in the middle there you are looking with-it and well organised.

The first example of this relationship overlap stratagem was my marrying and impregnating Anne Boleyn whilst still technically married – though working on the fine print – to Catherine of Aragon.

The next and better example of this winning strategy – one that makes even me impressed with me – is the day after Anne Boleyn's beheading, I officially announced my betrothal to Jane Seymour.

We were married eleven days later.

Like a boss.

Wait, say you who did not read *Wolf Hall*, who is this Jane Seymour?

Ah, Jane Seymour. She was a beautiful, voluptuous five-layer Yum Cake, one of those cakes that is nearly all frosting and very little actual cake. She was more carbs, butter, and sugar than human.

Her face shone at my approach.

The lids of her eyes fluttered at my touch.

Her mouth snarl-meowed as my lips drew near.

She was an empty canvas of thought and opinion, waiting for my thoughts and opinions to give the life of her mind a swirl of color and radiance.

She was attentive.

She was dutiful.

She was what binge-eating aspires to be.

Jane had been at court for some time, first as one of Catherine's ladies-in-waiting and later transferring loyalties to Anne B, serving among her retinue of attendants as well. I truly hadn't noticed Jane until toward the end of 1535 when she was in her late twenties and I was in the frame of mind for some Lady Next.

I like to think that I opened my Advent calendar that December and out popped Jane like a holiday Snickerdoodle.

The two of us had been playing an increasingly lovely game of touch-this-feel-that in various stairways and narthexes since the end of the prior year or so. And then Anne had been arrested and that had rather cleared my schedule to spend quality seductory time with Jane.

Whereas Anne had taken the motto "The Most Happy," with its focus on her own emotional life, Jane's was "Bound to Obey and Serve" with an unambiguous emphasis on me. Nailed it.

As I said at the beginning of this digression, we were married less than two weeks after Anne had gone off to produce bat-winged girl babies with Satan in the fiery furnaces of Hell.

Everything was perfect and we danced and enjoyed each other's company immensely. Church bells rang out across the land at the notice of our wedding, sermons were preached on her virtue, the royalty of Europe sent word of congratulations – except the Pope obviously because he's a big, farty, odious, glistening pile of sheep's vom.

We feasted, we talked excitedly of our enjoined future, we knelt and thanked God for each other, and we did the booty bounce quite a lot in bed.

And then the perfect became perfecter. Jane was made pregnant. By me. As the result of things such as my sexy chat-up lines (like "Is that a male heir in your womb or are you just happy to see me?") and hot dance moves and alluring lute playing and erotic poems and the thing you do with the penis and so forth.

And then the perfecter became perfecterer.

Like if you could multiply perfect by however many numbers there are.

In October 1537 Jane gave birth to a boy.

A boy!

A boy!

A boy!

Edward VI!!!

My brilliant overlap strategy had worked and I now had a healthy male Tudor heir at last. Only one mind you. It's always prudent to have at least two but one is a lot more than zero.

Life was a rampage of happiness.

And it was whilst holding that little man heir in my arms that I learned happiness is nearly always the music cue for disaster to make its entrance.

And so it was, mere days after delivering from her body, the heir England had been insisting upon, Jane Seymour died.

What a shitty thing to do to me.

Did she check in with me first?

No.

Did she communicate with me on this? Like, at all?

She did not. And communication is the foundation for any good relationship. Communication and hating the same things and people, actually. Shared distain and abhorrence is a bigger deal than is commonly recognised.

Jane's unexpected exit left me to seek empty solace with lonely widows, lusty laundresses, randy shepherdesses, ladies-in-mating and the odd foreigner who exhibited most if not all the key attributes of femaleness.

I say, empty for purposes of heightened drama, because really, is sex ever empty? There are in my experience three basic types of rumpity pumpity:

1. Really, really great sex that leaves you thinking that if there is no heaven that's actually okay.

2. Sex that is quite lovely but does not inspire shouts of admiration or the calling upon of God and his glory or sonnets afterwards or the purchase of jewels or even the offer of a sandwich. It simply does the job and everyone is rather pleased.

3. Sex that happens, happens in silence, and feels like something's not quite right. In these cases one finds that one has partnered with a piece of furniture, a book, or some sort of taxidermy and one is drunk. Even so, it is not without merit.

What We Have Learnt in Chapter 27
- Overlap
- Overlap
- Overlap
- Sex with books happens

Chapter 28

More Erotic Tudor Poetry

Is there anything to oil the chute toward the making of love than poetry? Only perhaps alcohol or money. Here are more original works of poetry, written by me, sure to stoke the fire of one's loins. Transcribe each on a card and read them aloud to an intended. Naked things will come to pass.

I taste your mouth
I think you ate my bacon
I'll have you beheaded in the morning.

***

In the firelight
She watches my gown fall away
And gives a scream
Of joy
Or it's - ? Maybe it's - ?
No, it's joy.
It's totally joy. I know things.

***

Lying by the fire
Wearing only cakes & pies
Just looking at me will give you diabetes.

***

Roses are red
Violets are blue
Sometimes I have
Codpiece feelings for you.

Chapter 29
Awaken the Dazzling Poet-King Within (But Don't Literally Aspire To My Throne As I Would Need to Have You Slain, Just Saying)

Write tip: It's not plagiarism if you've had the original author boiled

People are often surprised when I Tudorsplain that there is a good deal more to my version of being a poet-king than simply knocking out world-class poetry. I wrote lots of catchy tunes as well including "Pastime With Good Company," which totally rocked Eurovision 1519! I am of course credited with writing the hit single "Greensleeves." And as it is widely believed, it is therefore true.

Before writing this book, I penned a brilliant little volume in 1521 titled *"Assertio Septem Sacramentorum"*, which is Latin for "How to Party Your Trousers Off Whilst the Wife is in Prison." Haha. OK. The real title in English is "Defence of the Seven Sacraments" in which I called Martin Luther a total festival of wank, and Thomas More did not write it for me. I wrote it. Every word. All of it. And if you have any questions along that line feel free to ask More. His current email address is: ThomasMoresHead@TowerBridge.co.uk.

I received a book award for that one. From the Pope – this is when we were still speaking. It was a "Defender of the Faith" trophy, which sits on my desk looking shiny and splendid. It is also a title, which I added to my long list of accomplishments and one which your Queen still claims among her many titles to this day. Because she's a baller.

There is much I could tell you, sweet reader, about the writing of poetry, verse, and prose. No doubt I could write an entire book on the subject but I won't because it's the sort of book that only would-be writers purchase and as such would likely make as much money as I lose in a day down my toilet.

Even so, there are things you can learn from even the briefest glimpse at my writing process.

For this successful poet-king, producing compelling, engaging, enlightening, scintillating poetry and prose, the sort that makes your brain feel like it's enjoying the best Olympic-level fornication of its life, is the result of a finely honed process.

Here is my daily writing process:
- bacon
- quiet contemplation (which involves shouting at people, mainly)
- nap
- more bacon
- more writing
- loads of pissing about on Twitter
- having some Papists burnt to clear the mind
- eating to avoid writing
- doing the crossword to avoid writing
- scouting Twitter for images of famous ladies' sideboob
- trying to decide who wore it better
- having sex as a way of both avoiding writing <u>and</u> conducting research on love and relationships
All of which has resulted in this book.

What we have learnt in Chapter 29
- Poets and kings have a shared interest in not spending a lot of actual time actually writing poetry
- inspiration lies within the process
- sideboob

Chapter 30
When your beloved makes that dark, deflating
journey from super hot to super not

*Tudor Love Tip: When your love life gives you
lemons, make that kind of lemonade that's mostly
alcohol*

It happens. We all know it. We see it. And
still something inside us withers when it actually
does, some light in us goes out. Why is it so
torturous to watch your beloved go from sizzling to
pizzling? Because it's a kind of death.

If you are fortunate enough, or young
enough, to have never witnessed this and need to
know what it's like, here you go. Imagine being
served a lovely 40-pound baked swan tricked out
with bacon, meat sauces, and cheesy breadcrumbs.
You take your first bite – glory! Your second bite –
dreamy! You take your third through 17th bite –
heavenly! But just before that 18th bite you watch
with a mix of horror and more horror as your feast
turns blue-green with mould and then black with
putrefaction, collapsing greasily before your eyes in
a cloud of morbid stench. Gone. Forever gone.

And for what good reason? None. None at
all.

You groan, you weep, you hurl furniture,
you smash your collection of tiny glass ponies (and
then wish you hadn't). You feel an exquisite
emptiness, brutal betrayal, and inky injustice that
are impossible to put into words except then you do.
It's like that.

We've already seen a few versions in my own life of this heartbreaking switch from burning and fiery to cold and ashy.

This can take many forms. Catherine of A collapsed in the sexy department because her dry, shrunken womb sucked the life out of the rest of her body (like a little vampire lodged inside her – creepy!). Annie Bee collapsed because she said mean things about my poetry and I stopped liking her and her womb was dead and sad. Janey S actually died. And now I would find yet another version of the phenomenon.

I needed to seek out the next love of my life. The European Continent was of course oozing with the daughters of this or that house of some important-sounding lineage. There were any number of candidates but the right one had to be a very special lady.

One afternoon Cromwell and I each created a vision board of the top attributes of the lady I should woo.

Onto his board Cromwell pasted pictures of:

- A serious-looking lady holding a naked boy baby in each arm while holy angels looked on
- A lady's shoe smashing a map of Europe (a bit weird, that – something about forming badass political alliances???)
- The Pope having wet his dress

My vision board was a collage of:

- A pretty lady and a king in a very attractive cape riding on a horse in a meadow and the king is shooting a stag and the lady loves him and the kingdom is cheering
- Bacon
- A turd lying on a map of Spain

134

- Hearts enwreathing a throne of pies sitting atop France
- A lady on her back firing babies from her womb at an England-shaped archery target
- A pretty lady and a fat king having sex on a rainbow
- The Pope exploding

Based on all this, Cromwell promised to find the lady of my dreams and political aspirations. But mostly dreams.

He reached out to Christina of Denmark, who it turns out was a bit too busy being a complete shit to be bothered. He then directed a search in the Low Countries and the German kingdoms and principalities, where they'd told the Pope to piss actually off. Cromwell became rather frantically fixated on a lady called Anne of Cleves, talking a lot of breathless bollocks about statecraft and stratagems and I finally thundered, "BUT IS SHE HOT?!?!?"

"Yes of course, your majesty," he said giving me his imitation of a smile, which I wished to strike right off his face.

"SHE HAD BETTER BE HOTTER THAN A THOUSAND SUNS!"

I used my caps-lock voice thinking this might have an effect. But when Cromwell didn't in the slightest seem affected by it I began to wonder if the magic of shouting had finally worn off. This can happen even to the most effective/brain-damaged leader. One must be on constant alert and ready to change tactics on a whim.

We sent my court artist Hans Holbein off to Germany to produce a portrait of this potential bride, which he did, returning with an image of a demure lady with virtuous downturned eyes though with every possibility of going after it HAMMER AND TONGS in the bedchamber. You know the sort. Frankly there was something about her youthful, soft-figured coquettishness that reminded me of a young, sex-kitten Catherine of Aragon and I felt myself stir. Yes, stir. With a very large spoon in my very large kettle.

I'll skip a lot of the logistical goings on and flyings about. But at long last her ship landed on the English coast and I was so eager to see this sprite of Europe, this dream of Cleves, this Teutonic orchid. To the surprise of all I impulsively hopped on a rather alarmed horse and splashed and thundered my way to the gloomy old castle where she was staying that first night.

I bolted into the room where she was standing stunned and Germanic and I beheld Anne of Cleves for the first time. With her beefy red nose, weak chin, and blubbery neck made of yeasty dough on the rise. Her eyes wide and protuberant, nostrils flaring. Like a rescue horse. And she had a weird odour as in cases where one kind of food has been stored too long next to another kind of food. Like duck that smelled distressingly of cod.

What did I do? If I had read a fantastic book called *Unleash Your Inner Tudor* I would have bloody well been focused (in a healthy way, obvs) on my needs, my goals, and my dreams and told her to pack herself within her own bum and get back on that bleeding ship.

But the book you are now reading was not, sorrowfully, available on local bookshelves and so I was destined to fart on and flail about. (Although to be fair there was a sort of audio version of the book available to me in my head.)

136

And so this was the new version of the hot-to-not phenomenon I mentioned at the start of this chapter. Thanks to Holbein's portrait the image in my mind was of a lovely, youthful, attractive, sexually available, completely serviceable and alluring thing, who would be eager to present to me her basket of yummy body parts for my pleasure-y pleasure.

The moment my eyes struck her actual form the image in my mind shattered like a mirror struck by a hammer.

YOU HAD ONE JOB ANNE OF CLEVES!

Everyone knows that a woman's only true job is to be sexy. And when they're not one senses that they're doing it on purpose, almost with pride and defiance, as though by their very resolute unsexiness telling you to piss off.

Be wary of the tenaciously non-sexy woman, sweet reader. Something about her has clearly come unhinged. She's not playing the game. She's like the weird, deranged actor who's gone off script.

I complained a good deal about Anne of C and frequently shouted out of windows, "I like her not!"

Privately I wept and smashed things.

Because Cromwell was no longer reacting to my tantrums, screams, and massive strops – what did I have to do to get a bitch to grovel? – to get his attention I ripped his vision board apart and had him hauled away to The Tower and hurled into a cell for the crime of not finding my dream lady.

Against all the voices inside my head that demanded justice, a firm hand, and hotness, I married Anne anyway (OMG I can only barely write these words!!) but I did not give her any pet names unless you count "Horse Lady" or "Man of Cleves", did NOT play slap-and-wangle with my heir-maker AT ALL, complained more frequently, and then commanded Archbishop Cranmer to have the marriage annulled.

Finally, to really get his attention, I had Cromwell beheaded.

(I've realised that some people are auditory learners, others are visual, whilst some only learn by being publicly executed.)

I thought about having Holbein beheaded as well for his atrocious and misleading portrait of Anne. I had the quill in my hand, I had the death warrant before me. But alas, I sighed, he's an artist, which means he's a complete idiot. It'd be like killing a squirrel for not knowing how to build London Bridge.

There are Five Stages of Grief When A Lady Goes Completely Non-Sexy:
1. Rage
2. Rage alternating with tears and moodiness and rage
3. Look for someone to blame/behead
4. Throw her off
5. Track her down and give her the gift of smoking-hot intercourse

I know, that last one is always a surprise. After Cromwell's execution I rode out to Hever Castle, (which I'd taken from Anne of B's remaining family and given to Anne of C) and maybe it was the country air, maybe it was the *esprit* of the springtime in my veins, maybe it was the garland of roses she hung lovingly on my codpiece – as though crowning me the King of May – when she met me at the gate. We shagged. We shagged in the gallery. We shagged on the stairs. In the kitchen. In the garden. In various antechambers. The serving women were weeping, the footmen appalled, the members of a local lute trio all showed signs of trauma. Four words:

- Could.
- Not.
- Be.
- Helped.

After Cleves had been publicly humiliated by my tantrums, had humbly and dutifully borne a great deal of scorn and ridicule and had accepted the Cranmer-engineered annulment with grace and dignity, I totally wanted her. I wanted her in the worst way. Which is, of course, the best way.

I didn't want her enough to marry her. I was 1000% fine to be Friends With B's for I already had my eye on my next smoking hot bit of buttock/wife.

What We Have Learnt in Chapter 30
- Don't let your friends pick who you shag/marry
- Artists are dumb as rocks
- When rogered in secret, ugly ladies are amazeballs

Chapter 31
Food Loves You Back

Tudor Life Tip: That sad empty place inside of you is where meat, cheese, and alcohol are meant to go.

Feelings. I spent decades confused as to why God would give us feelings when we already had so many prickly and incoherent things to deal with such as wives and daughters. Why layer upon life's great steaming heap of challenges these diaphanous, invisible bits that float about in our minds turning a perfectly lovely moment sour?

Rage I can understand. Rage gets things done. Fear is good too so long as it's inside other people and I have inspired it. A very effective leadership tool. Confidence – the perfect feeling really. The king of feelings. The only one worth having. Other than aggression, obviously.

But wistfulness? What's the bloody point of wistfulness? Or desolation? Desperation? Boredom? Resignation? Or confusion? OMG, that one's the worst.

I do count myself fortunate to be physically incapable of experiencing the following:
- regret
- shame
- embarrassment
- remorse

These are weak feels felt only by weak people and serve no purpose AT ALL – other than to get in the way of glory, greatness, and feeling good about your accomplishments. Do you think Alexander the Great, Catherine the Great, or anyone else whose last name was Great EVER felt bad about ANYTHING? (The only possible answer to that rhetorical question is no, btw. Don't make me write another quiz!)

Out of his immeasurable love, God took these from me with my blessed jousting injury/brain repair. If I felt them in the past, I have absolutely no memory of them now. (I doubt that I did but my editor keeps telling me that I need to be more "relatable" especially if we hope to get a Netflix deal.) They are mere words as disconnected from my interior emotional life as is most of Portugal.

Indeed that last great jousting injury was the shower of gifts that kept on giving. In addition to everything else, it forced upon me a period of rest, during which I was once again able to hear the voice of the Holy Heavenly Completely Amazing Lord God Jehovah showing me the way forward.

There I was one afternoon in my bedchamber ensconced in a pillow fort on my bed in an utter state – simultaneously outraged with (pre-beheaded) Cromwell, shouting at the Papal Envoy, annoyed by daughter Elizabeth, scandalized by Scotland, and vexed by a host of other problems – when, behold, @Tudor_Cook sent up a cake from the kitchen to my bedchamber. It was a thing that was fully unasked for and a completely lovely gesture; A shaft of afternoon sunlight struck it just as it was being ferried through the door.

The serving men thought to place the cake on a table near the window but as I was clearly unable to rise they very hesitantly brought it to my bed.

Which is when four words came floating across the skies of my mind as though made of rainbows and unicorn parts:

A cake in bed.

I was about to enjoy – a cake – in bed.

141

An entire cake.

All to myself.

In my bed.

The very idea – its simplicity and perfection – sent a frisson of jubilation through me.

Once it rested on my lap, I ordered every person from the room. Somehow I knew this moment – the purity of this moment – could only be fully appreciated alone. Just me and the family of mes inside of me. And once it was just my majesty, my cake, and my sunny English late afternoon, I tucked in and felt, within seconds of the first wave of sugar and simple carbs hitting my mouth, my mood transform and lift into one of total elation. All troubles gone. All turmoil vanished. For the eight minute that it took to consume the entire cake, the inside of my being felt like it had floated on a pillow to a pretty cloud where lived joyful, uncomplicated, undemanding, 18-to-27 year old single ladies.

As I lay back against my pillows following this gorge-y orgy, I experienced that kind of swept-away pleasure and gratification one only senses after a job well done. A thing accomplished. A battle won. A neighbouring country invaded. An heir properly made.

As there is no word for this feeling in the English language I've come to call it simply "That moment when it's like you're the Loch Ness Monster astride a flying lion whilst painting the Mona Lisa, shooting lightning from your eyes, and sexily strumming a lute." (I'll bet the Germans have a 27-letter word for this emotion with 42 consonants, three different choking noises, and an umlaut.)

It was then, in that very moment of cake-y afterglow, that I heard the words of the Lord whispered gently into my ear saying, "This is what love is supposed to feel like but so often doesn't."

Srsly. Who wouldn't wipe a tear at a moment like that?

Wow.

I said, "Thank you sweet Jehovah for giving unto me, your humble servant, this ever-present source of love-substitute."

This moment was as life changing, as life re-defining as the one when Anne Boleyn's mum jumped me when I was 15. I knew that nothing would ever be the same. I had been baptized in the river and was born anew.

They say that the journey of a thousand miles begins with a single step. Which is weird, apparently this is how peasants travel? Why would anyone travel that far on foot? If I'm going on a journey of that length, any length really, the first step is to sit my spectacular arse in a big, gold-leafed carriage and wave at throngs of cheering subjects whose unkempt, greasy, tax-paying faces pass by my window.

Point is, so often every great undertaking begins with something modest and underrated. In this instance that cake in bed was something like the first blind date in what would turn into a loving, committed, lifelong relationship with binge eating.

The Tudor Mood-Food Matching Game
Test Your Knowledge!
When it comes to transforming a bad mood into a good one, love works and so does sex but sadly neither is ever available when you really need them. Food (and I include alcohol here) is the one thing

you can count on in this world to manage your feelings. Below match the pointless feelings in mood column with the food that most effectively changes that mood into happiness.

MOODS	FOODS
Apprehensive	Roast boar
Betrayed	Tarts
Blue	Boiled eels
Bored	Beaver tail
Cautious	Cakes
Cranky	Ale
Dejected	Roast beef
Depressed	Block of
cheese	
Despair	Meat pies
Distressed	Bacon
Frazzled	Roast hen
Grudging	Honey
Hurt	Cheese pies
Ignored	Porpoise
Jealous	Wine
Lonely	Duck
Merciful	Heron
Needy	Cod
Panicky	Breads
Provoked	Biscuits
Shaggered	Treacle
Sorry	Sweet meats
Troubled	Oxtail soup
Unhappy	Pheasant
Yearning	Lamb

ANSWERS: Congratulations on a perfect score! The exciting news is that our Lord has made this matching business easy (and I only included this overlong list of foods and moods to pad out the page length and give my book a sexier girth). All food – *except vegetables* – in large amounts has the ability to transform a bad feeling into a good one. Some may work better than others for you (bacon), so experimentation is a must! Plus, in your era, you have even more options than those of us in the 16th century such as gin and Nutella.

I think we should end this chapter on a poem:

Roses are red
Violets are blue
Only pies, cake, and wine
Will always love you

What We Have Learnt in Chapter 31
- Love, sex, and binge-eating are three sides of the same coin
- Sit in bed and eat cake until you're happy again
- If God is love, and love is cheese, then God is cheese (mind blown!)

Your Tudor Weekly Plan

Saturday:
- Bacon
- Say things that sound important
- Give every appearance of thinking important thoughts
- Back up threats with violence
- Beg God for heirs but in a cool totally non-needy way
- Cake

Chapter 32
On the Wooing, Winning & Bedding of a Lady
Who is As Old As You Feel on the Inside

Tudor Love Tip: When someone else's happiness is your happiness, that's love. Or emotional enslavement. They're very nearly the same.

There comes a time in every person's life, during the march down the chilly, chalky staircase to the tomb, when you realise that something weird has happened. You are no longer one age but two.

Here's what I mean.

When you are 12 years old, all of you is 12. When you are 18, your entire being is 18.

But by the time of your, say, 52nd birthday, you come to the odd discovery that somewhere back in the past something inside you split.

Your skin is indeed 52 years old.

Your hair and beard are 52.

Your ball bag is 52.

But your mind is 18.

Your heart is 18.

Your soul is 18.

And thus when it comes time to select a new spouse you find you have a choice – to woo and acquire a lady who is the age of your fallen neck or one who is the age of your brain or some other piece of your bloom-of-youth anatomy.

And let's be honest, most people really, really, really prefer someone a lot younger than their skin. Maybe even the tiniest bit younger than their minds.

It's how old you feel inside that counts. Am I right?

Women try to deny they possess this urge for a brain-age partner, claim they don't have such feelings, but I happen to know this is complete bollocks. Women are people (look how enlightened I am) and people at all points in life quite like to make the Writhing Wreath of Rogerment. And they like it with someone who's hot. Full stop.

After the debacle(s) of my first four marriages, I was ready to laugh. Relax. Enjoy my days showered by gentle affection, sweet whisperings, and the blustery-thrustery of making a male heir or two. Or five. By this point thanks to my committed and loving relationship with food I was heroically and gorgeously obese, was rocking the diabetes, rocking the gout, rocking the malaria (yes doubters we have malaria in 16th-century England) and rocking the personality disorders. Oh, and I was the owner of a suppurating leg wound that needed to be drained and repacked by a team of doctors on the daily. Oh, and I drank a lot. If you were to sum myself up in a single word it would be: fun. And confident. And sexy. Okay, that was four or five words. I cannot be contained in a single word like a nut within a shell.

Whilst theoretically still married to Anne of Cleves my loving eye fell upon a sweet English lass named Kathryn Howard, who was about 15 or 16, thereabouts, and whom I called my "rose without a thorn". Which meant of course that I expected this latest romantic overlap would be all beauty and no pain. Hilarious. Anyway. The moment her eyes met mine you could feel a high wattage hum – and this was centuries before wattage was invented so you know it was serious.

There she was in a window seat at Hampton Court doing needlework. Head bent, intent on her design, sunlight setting the back of her glossy white neck aglow.

"My lady," I said to her.

She rose awkwardly and gave me a quick kneel. With both knees bent as is my preference. Nailed it.

"Your Great and Glorious Majesty," she responded in a voice of utter "whatever you're looking for, it's all right here, baby."

I took her hand and watched a visible shiver of pleasure pass through her.

Pretty sure it was pleasure. To be fair it may've been pleasure mixed with something else. Like anticipation or. Elation, probably.

I turned to the gaggle of noblemen, diplomats, clergy, musicians, clerks, and servants who had been trailing me down the gallery and announced, "Gentlemen we have here my next mistake of historical proportions!"

This was followed by warm applause, cries of "Hear, hear" and a jubilant round of "For He's a Jolly Good Fellow".

Kathryn did not make eye contact with me, for she wasn't allowed to just yet, but I saw that she raised her face to the assemblage and gave a wan smile.

In retrospect she was being pretty seductive in a sort of laconic, not-laying-it-on sort of way.

Later that night I had her called to my chamber where I had to insist that she actually look at me. She played at reluctance like any good subject would but she eventually gave in.

When our eyes locked, wow. Just wow. No words. Well, wow is a word. But other than wow no other noun, adjective, intensifier, or interjection would do.

I took her small hand and that same sort of twitchy reaction of elation went through her like a seizure. She clamped her other hand to her mouth as though to stop her lips from actually crying out. In joy.

"You are so very beautiful," said I.

"Thank you, Your Majesty."

Her eyes glazed. No, sorry. Scratch that. Her eyes blazed.

I wanted her. I had to have her. But the clock of mortality was still ticking and whilst I wished to be gentlemanly and to woo properly, I also needed to get down to business.

I leaned close and said quietly, "You're of course a virgin."

Her eyes had a pleading look. How she wanted me.

"Ah, well on that point, Your Gloriousness," she began, "Technically –"

"I knew you were," I said, a smile spreading across my face. "I'm king. I know things, my sweet lady."

"But –"

I placed a finger gently to her lips.

"Shhhhhh. We don't need words. You and I only need our hearts."

"Wait. Just our hearts? That's it?"

"We are in love, are we not?"

Kathryn was so moved at this she placed her hand to her mouth again and spun away from me.

Is there any joy greater than that of bringing joy to others?

Do I need to answer that? I was being rhetorical. OK. There literally might be a joy greater than that but I can't think of it at the moment.

Wait. I've just thought of one but it's a bit random and will spoil the flow in this part of the book. So. Whatever.

Kathryn Howard.

Though today, I know –

So it was eating a pie with your hands and you're in France and you're drinking wine and you get the news that your army back home, under your wife's command, has totally destroyed the Scots at Flodden and their king is dead and you're just about to have sex with a French lady you found in a village. That is the greater joy I was thinking of.

OK. Back to Kathryn Howard.

Though today I know you have a lovely Castle Howard where you film iconic images of English nobility, Kathryn hailed from a lesser, darker, more cobwebby side of the family, her father being a second or third son who, through the magic of single-mindedness and alcoholism, sired something like 20 children. So perhaps not the dewiest of English flowers but fair and pretty and pleasing to the eye and to my nibbly bits that like to go rawr. The fact that she was Anne Boleyn's cousin should have come with a lot of loud cellos doing screechy foreshadowing music, I suppose, but somehow it did not.

Kathryn tried to keep me in the friend zone as a lady was supposed to do in that era but eventually of course there came the night when I called her unto my bedchamber.

There I was twice her height, three times her width. She climbed into the vast kingly bed for the first time and I took her litheness in my arms and there was a brief awkward/romantic moment when her head got caught under that large, wiggly flap of flesh I have under my armpit. She pretended she

151

couldn't breathe and that's when I gave her the pet name of Suffo-Kate.

I was again made happy.

Because I had not yet truly learnt that the happiness of a relationship is the first chapter in a book titled "What to Expect When You're Not Expecting Catastrophe".

The thing that has been bringing you such joy will rather suddenly stab you violently in the heart whilst simultaneously attacking your balls with a chair.

Somewhere in my soul, from the moment I saw her doing needlework I knew that Kathryn Howard was A VILE TART!!!! Yes, all-caps with four exclamation marks; I'm not simply being dramatic. I do so strive for accuracy. Is that what secretly attracted me to her? Of course not. That would make me a perv. How dare that sentence even appear in this book. It's an outrage.

It would be a good time right now, dear reader, to thank Jehovah himself that you have this book in your possession and that you can learn lessons of great importance from the abuse that I endured.

5 STEPS TO VILE TART SPOTTING

1. They are often suspiciously comely and young and manage to be where your eye is.
2. They are overtly attractive and have all of their teeth. Now their poison is in you!

3. Prior to meeting you, they perform unspeakable acts with someone who is not you! In my case it was some git named Francis Dereham and when I say unspeakable I mean they had sex. Probably

more than once! Partially to not-partially clothed! In a bed!

4. Before your marriage you believe them to be pure and virginal and are almost completely certain that they told you so even if you can't quite remember on which occasion this false assertion was made. But it was probably in moonlight when they were talking and you couldn't quite hear them because you were eating a duck.

5. They say they love you, they say you are their one and only; they marry you, and then tart off with some other fellow. Kathryn violated our marriage vows by playing sucky face and sucky wiener and squishity-slappity-suckity-knicker-bits with a servant in my court named Thomas Culpepper.

What To Do With A Vile Tart When She Is Your Wife – And You're Me
When you're my wife, you're married to England. It is England who bejewels and bespangles you, England who caresses your cheek and calls you its mouse, England who makes sweet, sweet love to you (or maybe at you, or in your general direction), and England who willingly sleeps in the wet spot. And England was not even microscopically amused by Kathryn's dalliances with Francis Dereham or Thomas Culpepper. The Privy Council was outraged. Parliament was livid. I was traumatised – for about three seconds. And then I knew instantly what to do. I almost sent for the Swordsman of Calais, as I had with Anne Boleyn, but let me tell you something that Cromwell got right. You don't want to repeat yourself – you want to stay fresh, #stayinspired – so after considering

having her burnt (always an option) or crushed under a great boulder or torn apart by bears or hurled from a high tower whilst on fire and then torn apart by bears on the way down, I decided for the more traditional English woodsman-y approach.

What To Do With A Vile Tart When She Is Your Wife – And You're You

Let's say that, hypothetically, you find yourself wedded to a VILE TART and you are not Henry VIII and do not hold sway over Parliament nor have the Tower of London at your disposal nor any henchmen. Not even one. Not even a dodgy Hungarian mercenary with syphilis. In that case ... bugger, well there's always drinking your troubles away, and eating platter of assorted meats and cheeses is nice (see earlier chapter on food-mood connexion) and of course paying your taxes is an excellent way to change your focus, but really beyond that ...

OMG being a peasant is so bloody uncinematic.

To finish. Kathryn was led away to have her head rendered free of her person on Tower Green and I think there are two points worth making. Today if you visit this place, someone has erected a memorial to those executed there. It is a frosted glass atrocity, which apparently passes for art in your era. Ghastly. Far more ghastly than actually witnessing a beheading unless of course it's the beheading of the tit who commissioned the piece in the first place.

The second bit has to do with that television show called *The Tudors*. Seen it? You know the part where Kathryn is about to be beheaded and she gives a moving speech about her abiding love for Culpepper? That didn't happen. HA! I WIN!

What We Have Learnt in Chapter 32
- VILE TARTS are out there, people, looking youthful and glorious, on the prowl for new victims all the time – be on your guard!
- What you do about the VILE TART in your life is likely subject to the laws in your region and/or principality and may also depend on your willingness to break those laws
- Showtime makes shit up

Chapter 33
Four Tudor Rules Governing Divorce (or in my case ANNULMENT)

So yes, there is that savagely ridiculous song about my wives that goes, "Divorced, beheaded, and died, divorced, beheaded, survived." People love to post that verse on my Twitter account all the time and it makes me bite into the nearest tapestry. The accurate version would of course be, "Annulled, annulled and beheaded, and died, annulled, beheaded (and forgot to annul – bugger!), survived." It requires a more complex rhythm scheme and music but being simple is not my superpower.

However, you must pick your battles in life and I doubt you lot will be won over by reason, so I now present my *Unleash Your Inner Tudor* divorce hacks (though be aware that when I write divorce with my pen, in my mind I am thinking annulment in my head).

1. When you think it's over, it's truly bloody over

The basic truth about marriage is this: remember the rule about fairies? The one that says the moment you stop believing in them they die? Your marriage is like that – a gleaming castle of delusion constructed upon an island of sparkly unicorn bollocks. The moment you think it's false and a chimera and a mirage and a hocus-pocus, it is all of those.

To my everlasting credit, what I took from that first nuptial experience, I applied to the others.

2. When it's over, never speak of it again

Nothing is more appalling than yammering on and on about your former marriage and your ex marriage partner. NOTHING IS WORSE – not even the sight of a donkey rotting in a tree or finding the beak of a chicken in your lover's underpants or accidentally watching a One Direction video. Nothing. Besides, not talking about it will make you look cool, like in a movie when Dwayne The Rock Johnson strides manfully away from an exploding medical supply warehouse (that's actually the secret global headquarters of a cabal of evil botanists) and he doesn't flinch or turn around.

3. Try to eradicate all evidence that your divorced spouse ever existed

As my love for Anne Boleyn died, I looked about and realised that I had surrounded myself with romantic emblems of her name and mine, the entwined H and A. Over archways, on paneling, on beds, on doors. HA. Tables. HA. Chairs. HA. Everywhere I went HA, HA, HA, HA, HA, HA, HA – a kind of hideous diabolical laughter no matter which way I turned deriding the very idea of love.

In her case, and those who came after, I had their emblems chipped off all the walls and entryways and all the various places they might appear. I burnt letters, destroyed portraits, jumped up and down on their favourite hats. Do whatever it takes, sweet reader; it's worth the effort and makes your heart feel whole again.

4. Revenge

I have oft heard it said that "to live well is the best revenge" but I still find that I prefer actual revenge.

What We Have Learnt in Chapter 33

- Never show fear in the face of movie explosions
- Don't stop believin' hold on to that feelin' … until believin' is just kind of stupid
- I was once rather appalled to see a rotting donkey in a tree and cleverly worked that image into the body of this book

Chapter 34
On Being the World's Most Amazing Single Dad

Tudor Parenting Tip: Raise your kids to be rude, self-centred, demanding, thoughtless, cruel little bastards and you prepare them for leadership.

With the untimely death of my fifth wife, I found myself single again and obviously a parent struggling through the rearing of three children with only the aid of dozens of servants, councillors, footmen, ladies-in-waiting, and all the gold in the English treasury. So, I get you, single parent. I understand your struggle. When I salute my own efforts at being a totally gifted and hard-working single father, I am saluting you. Probably.

My odyssey of single-dadness went like this. Cat of A gave birth to Mary, who from the start gave me nothing by threatening glares and rude mutterings under her breath. And she was a girl. Not the ideal heir obviously. Then came my mistress Bessie Blount who delivered unto me a boy, whom I named Henry Fitzroy, who as a bastard was also not an ideal heir but at least he had all the ingredients to fill a codpiece. So there was that. Anne Boleyn who, in her excessively insolent fashion gave me only a girl, my odd ginger daughter, Elizabeth. Then Anne died of unnatural causes and soon after so did Henry Fitzroy. FFS. Now I was back to having two girls.

Then came the beautiful and awesome Jane Seymour who gave me Edward VI, then she croaked.

Anne of Cleves gave me nothing but long, boner-less nights (except later as discussed). And Kathryn Howard was a VILE TART!!!!

So these were the cards Jehovah had dealt me. And why?

Likely it had to do with his greater glory. The Lord is all about bigging up his glory. (Praise him!) Too, they say that God never gives you more than you can bear. Which is true unless you're being hanged, drawn, and quartered.

Oh, and being eaten alive by crocodiles. Quite bad.

Being impaled is, I am told, incredibly nasty.

When you think about it, God dishes out things all the time that are more than anyone could possibly bear.

So it was with a deep sigh and an uncharacteristic feeling of uncertainty, I pulled a sheaf of vellum out of my desk and rated my children in order of how much I liked them and therefore who would be heir to my throne. The list went like this:

ROYAL SUCCESSION

1. Edward VI

2. Any other male heir(s) I might have with some other nice lady as the result of my stunning virility between now and the time of my so-called death

3. Might insert another name here at some point in the future

4. There could be a number four, you never know

5. Keep options open

6. There's likely a male cousin I'm forgetting

7. Perhaps one of those babies who're born with male and female bits, but whom we'd call a boy

8. Bloody Mary

9. Oh, look, they've brought me more cake!

10. Elizabeth

Children like to know where they stand with you. Well, at least Eddy liked knowing where he stood with me. The other two didn't. But girls don't like anything. How can you please the un-please-able? You can't. You must simply direct your energies elsewhere. (I do hope you're taking notes.)

The other thing I've learnt is that it is important for children, especially when you're a parent with a job, to try to connect with them at bedtime. Just try to spend a few minutes really reaching across the chasm of adult and child, parent and off-spring, king and potential assassin. (Do, though, limit this time to no more than a few minutes. Any more makes you look like a try-hard.)

To this end, I wrote a little rhyming ABC book that I could read to them each night before they nipped off to dreamland.

The Glorious Henry VIII Nighttime ABCs Book For His Various Children

A is Annulment, I awarded myself

B is Boleyn whose head's on my shelf

C is for Cromwell who's no longer healthy

D's dissolution, which made me quite wealthy

161

E is Elizabeth my odd second daughter

F is my Fame that gets hotter and hotter

G is for Greensleeves, I wrote to get tail

H is for Heir (see also "Male")

I is a pronoun of glory and grace

J is the Joust where a lance smashed my face

K is for Katherine, a name I wed thrice

K's also for King and that's me and that's
nice

L is for Love, which left my heart bleeding

M's for Male, which my dynasty's needing
(& why I go on piously breeding)

N is for Nonsuch, a palace I built

O is Obesity for I eat at full tilt

P is for Popes those wrinkly old pricks

Q is for Queen, I've had five or six

R is for Rex, that's Latin for King

S is for Spain, a great ugly thing

T's Tudorlicious, a word I just quilled

T's also for Tower where traitors are killed

U is the Union 'twixt a man & his wives

V's Vile Tarts who ruin our lives

W is Wolsey, a scoundrel & rapist

X crosses itself (and is probably Papist)

Y is the Ypocras I drink with my meat

Z is for Zebra, which I'd quite like to eat

So, the *Unleash Your Inner Tudor* childrearing hack – while I did show each child some kindness and gave them loads of sparkly royal things, the thing you must remember is that true leaders are so often motivated my miserable childhoods. Don't rob your children of their potential for greatness by making them happy. I raised three of England's greatest monarchs – how can I be wrong? I can't. No need to answer. Or if you must truly respond perhaps you could spend three years writing your own book called *Unleash Your Inner Unimportant Person.*

What we have learnt in Chapter 34
- Being an amazing parent means being there for the children who obviously like you
- Happy kids become happy adults who accomplish NOTHING in the tyranny department
- Cheerful bedtime poetry

Chapter 35
The 16th Century – a fantastic time to be a woman!

Tudor Lady Tip: I encourage all my wives to live every day like it's their last.

Although all I know of your era is what I read on Twitter, it is obvious that in my era women are far better off. Much of this is because there are so many fewer demands on them.

In the 16th century a woman is, first, the possession of her father and later the possession of her husband. And when I say possession, I don't mean like in some poorly acted-out S&M game that lurches on for 40 minutes on a Friday night with black vinyl, a tennis ball, and a strap. I mean something you own – like a plough. Or an ox. Or a box of turnips.

As such it is a vastly simplified life. There is order and duty and civility. In my century one does not see news stories such as, "Can Women Really Have It All?"

No.

They can't.

Sorted.

Nor are there books such as *Owning Your Orgasm*.

Women are forbidden from owning anything unless they have a husband or male relative as a co-signer. Not bloody likely.

Nor are there any magazines with names such as *Take a Break* as "taking a break" doesn't exist (unless you mean a break from Rome) or *Real Simple* as things could not be simpler.

We could possibly have magazines with names such as *Woman's Own* (except they can't own anything) *Real Honouring Your Husband* or *House Dutiful*. Likewise there might an audience for a book called *Our Bodies, Our Smells* – but again, women aren't taught to read so where's the point?

Why do I say my era is better?

Is it just because I'm blinded by being a man and therefore superior?

No. Okay, perhaps, but no.

Is it because I think women are inferior to men?

They are, but no.

It's because women tell me all the time how wonderful and terrific and brilliant it is to be my wife and/or mistress and/or nice lady I happen to be in a bed with, on a cart, or near a sheep pen.

There are vastly important reasons that God gave men the job of running everything. Take warfare as a good example. What amazingly useful weapons do we use to fight and win wars? The sword, the arrow, the lance, the mace, the gun, and the cannon. Big reveal: these implements of conquest are all shaped like penises. And in the case of newer weapons – rifles and canons and such – they not only look like a dong, they actually mimic the workings of one, spewing a violent orgasm of victory. Now what kind of world would this be if all of our weaponry were vagina inspired? Imagine trying to kill a Spaniard with a mossy box or invading France armed with tacos.

Warfare is but one example of many – how about the arts and letters. Picture the great Michaelangelo trying to paint his Sistine Chapel with a clam? Or the noblemen of 13th century

England trying to write the Magna Carta with an orchid?

I could go on.

What We Have Learnt in Chapter 35:
- Simpler ladies = happier ladies
- Things with weiner shapes win wars
- Crap-ton should be a unit of measurement

Chapter 36
On Wooing a Lady Who Puts Up the Hilarious
Pretence of Perhaps Not Wishing to Be Yours

*Tudor Love Tip: Make her feel special. Yes she may
be your 5th or 6th wife but make her feel like she's
your 2nd or 3rd.*

In matters of love and loss, one must look
upon the beheading of a once-adored teenage wife
not as a problem but as an opportunity. In this
instance I had the chance to take up the role of
merry widower (once more), a part I played with
glee. At court we threw countless masques,
disguisings, feasts, pageants, and dances. It's never
too late to be happy, single, and beautiful.

But England was ever in need of more boys
who sprang from my splendid loins. Thanks to Jane
Seymour's womb – and my glory – the nation now
had young Edward VI to look to for future
leadership and awesomeness. But in the Tudor
family the need for a second, if not third in line,
should be beyond obvious.

Both Parliament and my Privy Council were
huffing and spittling themselves over the issue of
my issue. The realm would be more secure, they
pestered night and day, if there were more little
Henrys running about the palace, ready to fight each
other for the throne.

"No pressure, good sir!" I would shout at
my codpiece.

I was in my 50s, going a bit grey in the
beard, a bit thin of hair on the top. My ulcerated leg

that would not heal continued to not heal and so I was whisked about my palaces in a wheeled cart.

The Lord God "Noted Monarchist" Jehovah had seen fit to hold my lethal levels of sexiness in check with gout, diabetes, leg pain, headaches, and various mental disorders – probably wise. I was now wearing spectacles to read the tedious letters and threats and promises of false friendship from this or that king or ambassador. It was said that I was so huge that three big men could fit inside one of my shirts. I was a legend in my own time, the icon of my age, more myth than man. And my catchphrase was "Hey nonny nonny, bitches."

I remember gazing out the window of a coach one afternoon in Surrey and seeing two peasants shagging in a field. And being in a wistful frame of mind (an emotion I try to avoid) I lifted up my thoughts unto God and said, "Why, oh Lord, is it so easy for them? They're just bloody poor people."

And God replied unto me, "Oh, shut it, H! I do one nice thing for a couple of prols – get off my tits!"

He means well.

I now re-dedicated myself to the twin causes of ruling my kingdom with an iron fist and being an absolute delight to the ladies. I feasted the women of my court. Wrote songs for them. Dreamt up hot new dance moves. Flew out at them from alcoves when they least expected it. Fun.

I knew of course that my eye would eventually fall upon the lucky next Mrs. H. Tudor but realised I'd shoved myself into something of a jam jar. In order to have Kathryn Howard properly executed I'd smashed a bill through Parliament that said in essence, "If you, dear lady who are on the verge of marrying good King Henry (that's me), have done ANYTHING he should know about prior to your wedding – anything at all and especially those things involving a gentlemen manhandling your sacred bits – you must needs confess in full or your head shall be unfollowed by your body."

The ladies of my court were many things but virtuous was not one of them. So I'd managed to narrow the field rather perilously – to such a degree that as far as my councillors and I could tell the only candidates came down to Lady Catherine Parr and a 17-year-old girl with a withered hand and a pulpy eye living in Finland.

After picking my way through five marriages that involved disaster and death, it was best, I'd learnt, not to be led by your heart or with your codpiece, but to use a calm, reasoned, frontal-lobe sort of approach.

Catherine Parr was graceful, intelligent, and a good dancer. I enjoyed our banter together, our flirtations, and the thought of placing myself on top of her. Her only fault was that she happened to be married. Her husband, Lord Latimer, was, however, doing the nation the huge favour of dying just then, albeit at a pace that I found slow to the point of being unpatriotic.

As she sat at the bedside of her dying hubby, Catherine began to receive tokens of my affection and interest – gems, rings, poems, and pricey goblets with images of she and I frolicking naked in a forest with friendly dragons and monkeys. She let it be widely known that she was utterly dismayed at my amorous intent, which most people took seriously – because most people are too ignorant to realise there's this thing called satire. Pillocks.

Catherine was sophisticated and quick-witted and of course I knew instantly that she was pretending to be panicked and the very picture of consternation as a spoof on the popular idea that all I did for merriment was to have my wives executed.

Here's a poem I sent to her during this period:

That awkward moment when I'm falling for you
Whilst your husband is turning from pink to blue.
No one gets your humour like I do
Taylor Swift will steal that line someday – doo be doo be doo

Another month or two passed, Lord Latimer at long last died as we all hoped he would do and we mourned his pegging out in the most gracious ways possible. I was ready to swoop in like an eagle and collect my cute, furry lady-rodent.

Ah, but no. Now, I was told by my councillors that I needed to wait before putting my moves of hotness on Catherine Parr to ensure that I didn't look like a complete pig at the wench trough. In the meantime, it came to my attention that Thomas Seymour, brother of my lovely, dead Janey, was already hot on the prowl for Catherine. When you take the lid off the honey, how the insects drop in. So I had Seymour named to an ambassadorship in the Low Countries to keep him from sniffing around.

See how I did that?
- Husband – dead
- Competition - moved to Belgium
- Boom

Not long afterward, Catherine and I did indeed wed and things took an unexpectedly dangerous turn.

She was a wise, kind, generous, thoughtful, and age-appropriate bride – she was 31 and I was 53. It was all so without drama and scream fests and acrimony, she spoke to be gently and sweetly, that slowly I began to succumb to the venomous effects of boredom.

This is where the rational approach to love will get you.

It's horrible.

Of course I rallied. This is what a Tudor does. We fight!

Once I realised that I was being poisoned by Catherine's inherent decency, I instructed the captain of my guard to have her arrested and taken away to the Tower on some charge or other. I needed her out of my sight before she lured me to a ruinous end. He dashed off to get his men.

There I was sitting in the garden feeling in charge again, feeling flooded again with derring-do, manliness, and purpose, when who appeared at my side but Catherine herself. OMG. And she was so very pretty and charming and she used her soft, soothing, smart, boring lady voice on me and she wore her dress so nicely.

There was kindness and calmness in her voice. There was something about her that held the promise of the age of Henry VIII passing away and a new era for England, one that was less gingery and tyrannical. And it made me sad and weary.

It was the year 1547. I could feel something within me slipping away … away … away …

Christ, this was not cool.

She leaned close and now I could see the crease between her boobs. See how easy seduction is for ladies!! And I could no longer hear the actual individual words coming out of her throat but just the sane, bland, gracious, tedium of her voice. Lulling me toward the sweet arms of death.

Just then the captain of my guard showed up with his men to take Catherine Parr away and she looked at me with a look of such sorrow, as though she felt sorry for me and I shouted at the captain to leave my sight. I had no idea what he was talking about.

In that moment I knew I was done for. Here she was killing me with her goodness and I was defending her. Defending the creature that was sliding a benevolent and humane knife between my ribs and giving it a soft, womanly twist.

I simply crawled off to die.

Catherine came to my bedside and sobbed at the prospect of losing me. Anyone would. I could barely speak or move so incapacitate was I from the effects of the monotony with which her modesty, goodness and virtue had filled me to putrefying effect.

Little did I realise what was to follow.

What We Have Learnt in Chapter 36
- She wants you, of course she wants you, she's just being funny about it
- Eliminate your competition via the magic of death and/or Belgium
- The lady everyone says is so right for you, who will set you on the proper path, the one with whom you are a "cute couple", is the one who will probably kill you

Chapter 37
When Your Death is a Twitter Hoax

Tudor Death Tip: Prepare for the Ladies In Your
Afterlife to Be Just as Confounding and Full of
Complication As Ever

On January 27, 1547, I was going downhill
like a toboggan loaded with jolly, diabetic
Norwegians. My doctors kept bleeding me to get
my humours in alignment. My Master of the Stool
had rinsed me with unguents and ointments and
scented oils until my bum bits were like a garden of
May flowers. Nothing worked. Laughter, which
they say is the best medicine is not, I can say
definitively. I was dying. I signed my will, entrusted
my soul to Hippie Jesus, and uttered my final
words, which have been reported as "Monks,
Monks, Monks ..." Which is only partially correct
as I was actually working on a rap song that went
"Monks, Monks, Monks, I take your junks, junks,
junks away in trunks, trunks, trunks." It wasn't
perfect, alright? Did I say it was finished?

Anyhow, the end was nigh. I could feel the
icy fingers of death clutching me in places where
cold fingers do not belong. My kingdom – entire
communities, churches, counties, and coastlines –
filled with weeping supplicants raising their hands
skyward begging the Lord in his Mercy to spare
their king, this they beseeched with tears running
down their faces, torsos, and legs. Lying in my vast
and iron-reinforced bed, with noblemen who I had
not yet executed and clergymen who owed me their
lives and livelihoods, surrounding me with
appropriately grim and sad expressions, I felt
myself drift. 'Adieu,' I thought. 'Good-bye

wonderful Earth. I had such an amazing time thrusting my greatness upon you. I leave a fantastic legacy. I am a sexy 350 pounds (those last five are the hardest to gain, but I did it!), I look amazing on horseback, I've got smokin' hot dance moves, and no one looks better wearing only a crown.'

To everyone's amazement the following morning, I woke up feeling not bad at all and within just a few hours I had gotten to my feet and had deposited a blessed and monarchical poo in my velvet-and-tassel-covered chamber pot. By the next day I was feeling like sunlight on the sea – sparkly and beautiful. I went hawking with Brandon and on a dare ate the hawk, burped a feather and we fist-bumped. The king was back.

I had the Duke of Kent stuffed inside a goat skin and fired from a cannon – just to make a statement.

People on Twitter often ask (with undisguised snark!) how it is that I am alive and tweeting. The best explanation I can offer is this: when enough peasants shout "Good Save the King!" with the right sort of enthusiasm and actual feeling, God eventually listens.

So as you read this, my 16th Century lives on.

It's enormous fun. I win jousts and archery contests. I delight ladies where ere I go. I send rude letters to the Pope along with bottles of my urine (labeled "Tudor Chardonnay").

The only irritating bit is that as time goes on time itself gets wobbly-bobbly. Next thing I know Wolsey is trotting in with a treaty to sign. And he's not dead from the effects of financial ruin and exploding arse disease. Or worse, he and Cromwell burst in simultaneously with death warrants for me to sign for each other. The Duke of Kent who I shot from a cannon? He showed up again a decade or so later, no memory of being goat-stuffed and blown through the sky. Or I wake up in the wee hours beside Anne Boleyn – with her head attached, mostly – snuggling up next to me, jabbing my soft bits with her pointy bits begging to be the vessel for my male heir. Crikey.

Of late, just to stay in the game, I have taken up Mary Boleyn again. It was she who honoured one of my birthdays by giving me my Magic Twitter Box. Christ knows what warlock or scary witch person she got it from (I suppose I shall need to have her burnt). It is a small machine that I can hold in my hand. It is encrusted with jewels and has a lovely HRM at the top of it in filigreed gold. Upon the main body of the thing are big buttons (for big fingers) imprinted with letters and numbers. Images and words appear in a little window at the top. With it I have learnt all I know of your era and bits of what happened since my "death", which is obviously fake news.

But even Mary is capable of doing that lady-thing of throwing shade where shade is hardly required.

"You know, you've only got about 500 or 600 years to figure this out, don't you," Mary said to me recently, as she was stretched out in my bed. Warm afternoon sunlight scintillated through a window of my bedchamber. I was across the room wearing only gold underpants and a cape striking sexy poses, getting her in the mood.

"Oh do stop being opaque. You know I have people disembowelled for lesser things," I said.

"None of this will continue," she said, gesturing about, "unless –"

"Unless what!" I responded, approaching the bed. I believe her gesture took in more than our friends-with-benefits relationship, more than the palace, more than my kingdom itself, but in fact was meant to indicate the entirety of my after-life.

"It all vanishes unless you find love."

"Are you threatening me in some vague and irritatingly womanish way?!"

"I'm just saying that unless you find love, all of this goes away."

"BOLLOCKS!"

I seized my bedside broadsword and sliced off her head in a single, authoritative stroke.

Mary calmly reached for it and twisted it back on her neck.

"Not bollocks, Henny Penny. Law of the Universe," she said.

"Well that's it then, I'm not marrying you!" I boomed. "You'll not be wife number seven."

"Another dream crushed," she said mildly.

I paced about the room in an absolute turmoil. "How can you say, imply, or infer such a ridiculous idea! I have found love countless times! In countless ways! We are enjoying love at this moment!"

"Are we?" She smiled her beguiling smile.

"Of course!"

"Is this love?"

OMG, women. Even after-life women. With their bloody riddles and their pointless bloody complication. Never a moment's ease. I know all there is to know on all topics and especially on love! Love: what can I possibly NOT know about it?

Recall that I felt the inability to breathe, briefly, with Catherine of Aragon and went on being married to her long after I stopped wanting to be. I waited for six years to have sex with Anne Boleyn at tremendous cost to my mental health. I wept actual tears when Jane Seymour died without asking me if she could. I married Anne of Cleves when I didn't want to and I didn't have her beheaded when I it was clearly my prerogative. I had serious codpiece feelings for Kathryn Howard until I didn't. And Catherine Parr – I gave her the space she needed to bore me to death.

HOW IS THAT NOT LOVE!?

I've even felt sparkly, fizzily feelings for a few mistresses and even a lady I met once outside a water mill. Also, love. Obviously!!

And then there are the other sorts of love. I am the father of three children – who adore me. Well, except the girls, naturally, but that can't be helped.

And then there was the love I felt for my realm. You aren't the monarch every bloody hour of every bloody day of beloved England, Ireland, Wales and France – YES I SAID FRANCE! – without having some kind of feels about it.

And then there's food. Surely the emotions that take place in my mouth with meats, cheeses, pies, cakes and so forth can ONLY be described as the most sacred kind of love there is. Mouth-feelings are pretty bloody sacred!

So Mary B is talking complete pish-posh, twiddle-twaddle BALLS!!

I mean look what I have accomplished here. I have written this book to demonstrate the encyclopaedic nature of my knowledge of love – and a mindful and healthy lifestyle – in all its forms and disguises. While I'm at it – because of my love for you sweet reader whom I haven't met, haven't spoken to, haven't even seen naked – I have shared my amazing and completely useful tips on parenting, diet, leadership, and much more.

How is that not love?

However, there's a good deal that I don't know about the after-life just yet. Mary is completely wrong, obviously. But just in case, I get the feeling that if you, by reading this book, taking my invaluable advice to heart, and actually getting off your arse and finding love and perfecting your very nature, that will weigh very much in my favour – it will shut my critics and one or two unwelcome feelings in my heart up for all eternity!

Off you go.

No, wait. Take the bloody quiz first.

What We Have Learnt in Chapter 37:
- Death is not the end of fornication. Or love. Which apparently you're not supposed to use interchangeably.
- After-death mistresses: not the simple pleasures we'd like them to be
- During your soul-crushing search for love remember that it's apparently meant to be difficult and disappointing but there's no need to be emo about it.

Final Quiz

Have you learnt to *Unleash Your Inner Tudor*?
Take my royal and flawless quiz to find out.

1. If you're going to make mistakes, then at the very least do *what* whilst making them?
A. Burn bits of Scotland
B. Look amazing in your undercrackers
C. Eat a mallard

2. If you're a lady who is serious about wooing a gentleman, which of these is your most effective manoeuvre?
A. Place one of his hands on one of your sexy bits
B. Correct his grammar
C. Fart a little bit then blame an animal

3. If you're a man hoping to woo a lady, your move of ultimate hotness would be?
A. Become the tyrant of your own kingdom, wielding the power of life and death over your subjects and/or start your own church
B. Become a vegan
C. Have her mother over and serve soup

4. If the spouse who used to be hot becomes decidedly not, then your best recourse is?
A. Have "Not Hot" executed/ Find someone else to marry
B. Hurls Spaniards from the Tower
C. Turnips

5. The following is an example of what:
I want to be your overlord
And your under-lord.
Get it?

I want to have sex with you in more than one position.
Heat!

A. A passage from Cranmer's Book of Common Prayer
B. Tudor erotic poetry
C. Something that got scrawled on your face that time you got drunk and fell asleep on the train.

6. Henry VIII is:
A. The greatest monarch, father, warrior-poet, builder of navies, dancer, hunter, writer and mammal who has ever, or will ever, live on earth, breath air, occupy space and sit on the throne of any kingdom in the known or unknown universe
B. I want to be hunted down and killed

ANSWERS:
You probably got most of them wrong. Go purchase a second copy of the book and read it again. Repeat until you are the monarch of your own glorious island nation.

Epilogue
And now for the inspirational bit

Follow your heart, sweet reader. Even if it means
six marriages, a couple of beheadings and starting
your own major religion. Really. Focus on you.

***

One last erotic poem to make you feel squishy in
your squishy bits:

You are my boiled swan,
My cheese,
My eel pie,
My succulent roast beef,
You – sweet, sweet lady – are
my bacon
with boobs.

53733943R00113

Made in the USA
San Bernardino, CA
30 September 2017